SCHOOL
OF
THE SUN

Also available in the

SCHOOL
OF
THE SUN

Ana María Matute

TRANSLATED FROM THE SPANISH BY

ELAINE KERRIGAN

COLUMBIA UNIVERSITY PRESS

NEW YORK

Columbia University Press Morningside Edition 1989
COLUMBIA UNIVERSITY PRESS
NEW YORK

Originally published in Spanish under the title Primera Memoria
Copyright © 1959 Ediciones Destino
English translation copyright © 1963 by Random House, Inc.
Published by arrangement with Pantheon Books,
a division of Random House, Inc.
All rights reserved

Library of Congress Cataloging-in-Publication Data
Matute, Ana María, 1926–
[Primera memoria. English]
School of the sun / Ana María Matute ; translated from the Spanish
by Elaine Kerrigan.
Columbia University Press Morningside ed. p.   cm.
(Twentieth-Century Continental fiction)
Translation of: Primera memoria.
ISBN 0-231-06916-2 (alk. paper).
ISBN 0-231-06917-0 (pbk.)
I. Title.   II. Series.

PQ6623.A89P713   1963   88-36866
863'.64—dc19   CIP

Printed in the United States of America

Casebound editions of Columbia University Press books are Smyth-sewn
and are printed on permanent and durable acid-free paper

The Lord hath not sent thee; but thou makest this people to trust in a lie.

JEREMIAH 28, 15

Contents

THE *DESCENT*

MY GRANDMOTHER'S white hair was set in a bristling wave on her forehead. It gave her a certain angry air. She almost always carried a small gold-headed bamboo cane, which she did not need, for she was as steady as a horse. Looking over old photographs, I think I find in that thick, massive white face, in those grey eyes bordered by smoky circles, a glowing reflection of Borja, and even of me. I suppose Borja inherited her gallantry, her absolute lack of mercy. I, perhaps, my great sadness.

My grandmother's hands—big-boned, with prominent knuckles—though not lacking in beauty, were splashed with coffee-colored spots. On the index finger and on the ring finger of her right hand danced two enormous, dirty diamonds. After meals, she would drag her rocking chair to the window of her boudoir. The mist rose; the damp burning wind shook the pita plants, or pushed the brown leaves under the almonds; the swollen, leaden clouds obscured the brilliant green of the sea. From there, with her old opera glasses incrusted with false sapphires, she would scrutinize the white houses of the Descent, where the tenant farmers lived; or watch the sea, where no boat sailed, where no trace appeared of that horror we heard from the lips of Antonia, the housekeeper. ("They say that on the other side they are killing entire families, shooting priests and pulling out their eyes . . . and throwing others in vats of burning oil . . . God have mercy on them!") Without losing her inexorable air, her eyes closer together than ever, like two brothers confiding their darkest secrets, my grandmother heard the morbid descriptions. And the four of us—grandmother, Aunt Emilia, my cousin Borja and I—stayed there, saturated with heat, boredom, and solitude, anxious for some news that never was quite decisive enough (the war had begun scarcely a month and a half before), in the silence of that corner of the island, in that lost point of the world that was my grandmother's house. The siesta hour was perhaps the calmest, and at the same time, the most highly charged of the day. We listened to the creaking of the rocking chair in grandmother's boudoir, we felt her spying on the comings and goings of the women of the Descent, the grey sun blinking from the enormous solitaires on her fingers. Often, we heard her say that she was ruined; as she said it, she would pop into her mouth one of the infinitude of pills in brown bottles lined up on her commode, the shadows around her eyes deepened, and her pupils became enveloped with a gelatinous fatigue. She looked like a beaten Buddha.

I remember the mechanical movement of Borja, as he

rushed forward every time the small bamboo cane slid down the wall and fell to the floor. His large, dark, wide-knuckled hands,—like grandmother's—stretched towards it (the unique prank, the one protest, in the exasperating quietude of the siesta hour without a siesta). Borja rushed routinely, with the punctuality of the well-bred child, toward the rebellious cane, and set it back against the wall, the rocking chair, or grandmother's knees. On these occasions in which the four of us sat gathered in the parlor—my aunt, my cousin and I as audience—the only one that spoke, in a monotone, was grandmother. I believe no one listened to what she said, each one absorbed in himself or in his ennui. I watched for Borja's signal, which would indicate the opportune moment for escape. With frequency, Aunt Emilia yawned, but her yawns were of the closed-mouth type: they were only noticeable in the strong contraction of her wide, milky-white mandibles, and in the sudden tears which invaded her small, pink-lidded eyes. The wings of her nose dilated, and the grating of her teeth could almost be heard; her teeth, heavily pressed together so that she might not open her mouth all the way, like the women of the Descent. From time to time she said: "Yes, mamma. No, mamma. Whatever you say, mamma." That was my only distraction while I waited impatiently for the slight raising of Borja's eyebrows with which he would initiate our disappearance.

Borja was fifteen and I fourteen, and we were there against our will. We were equally bored and exasperated in the midst of the oily calm and hypocritical peace of the island. We had been surprised in the middle of our vacations by a war that seemed phantasmal: distant and close at the same time, perhaps more dreadful for its being invisible. I do not know if Borja hated grandmother, but he knew how to fake very well in front of her. I suppose since his earliest childhood someone had inculcated upon him the need for dissimulation. He was sweet and smooth in her presence, and thoroughly understood the significance of the words *inheritance, money, lands*. He was sweet and smooth, when it was convenient for him to appear that way before certain grownups. But I never saw as sly a rascal, liar, or traitor; nor anyone as sad. He feigned innocence, purity, and gallantry in front of grandmother, when, in truth—oh, Borja, now perhaps I begin to love you!—he was a pitiless, weak, and arrogant fragment of a man.

I do not think I was better than he. But I did not miss the occasion to demonstrate to grandmother that I was there against my will. And whoever has not been shunted from place to place and from hand to hand like an object, from the ages of nine to fourteen, will not be able to understand my disaffection and defiance at that time. Moreover, I never hoped for anything from my grandmother: I endured her icy treatment, her ready-made phrases, her prayers to a God of her exclusive invention and ownership, and even an occasional meaningless caress, as meaningless as her punishments. Her hands, speckled with pink and brown, would perch protectively on my head while she spoke, between sighs, with the two gossips from Son Lluch, about my corrupt father

(*infernal ideas, ominous deeds*) and my unfortunate
mother (*Thank God, she is in Glory*) on the afternoons
when the cats arrived at our house in their two-wheeled
carriage. (Their great hats were covered with musty
flowers and fruits, like leftovers, and the only thing
missing was a cloud of buzzing flies.)

I had been—she would say—a wayward and misdi-
rected creature, expelled from Our Lady of the Angels
for having kicked the sub-director; spoiled by a hostile
and foundering family atmosphere; victim of an unfeeling father, who, upon becoming a widower, abandoned
me to an old servant woman. I was—she continued, before the malevolent attention of the ladies from Son
Lluch—brutalized by the three years I spent with that
poor woman on my father's mortgaged farm, in a house
half-fallen to the ground. I lived, then, surrounded by
mountains and wild woods, ignorant and gloomy people,
far from love and protection. (At this point, my grandmother would caress me.)

"We shall tame you," she told me when I first arrived
on the island.

I was twelve years old then, and for the first time I
understood that I would stay there forever. My mother
had died four years before; and Mauricia—the old nanny
who cared for me—was brought low by illness. My
grandmother took definitive charge of me; there was no
alternative.

The day I arrived, it was very windy in the island city.
Some half-loosened signs rattled on the doors of the
stores. My grandmother took me to a dark hotel which

smelled of dampness and lye. On one side my room looked onto a small patio; and on the other it over-looked an alley, at whose mouth ran a promenade where palm trees rustled over a piece of leaden sea. The intri-cate, forged-iron bed frightened me, like a strange ani-mal. My grandmother slept in the adjoining room, and at dawn I awakened startled—as I often did—and searched, gropingly, with an arm outstretched, for the light switch on the night table. I remember well the cold of the stuccoed wall, and the pink lampshade. I was very quiet, seated on the bed, looking distrustfully around, amazed by the twisted shock of my own hair, standing out darkly against my shoulder. Accustoming myself to the darkness, I made out, one by one, the places where the wall was peeling, the large stains on the ceiling, and above all, the entangled shadows of the bed, like snakes, dragons, or mysterious figures I hardly dared to look at. I leaned over as far as I could toward the night table, for the glass of water; just then, in the corner of the room, I discovered a row of ants climbing along the wall. I let go of the glass, which broke on the floor, and I buried myself again between the sheets, and covered my head. I decided not even to put my hand out, and I lay like that a long time, biting my lips and trying to banish my des-picable tears. I must have been very frightened. Perhaps I thought I was completely alone: I was searching for something. I tried to think of something else, to allow my imagination to run like a little train through woods and familiar places, to get to Mauricia and cling to every-day images—the apples that "Mauri" had set carefully

on the planks, in the garret of the house, and the aroma
that invaded everything, to the point where, foolish as I
was, I pressed my nose to the walls to find out if they
had been impregnated with that perfume. And I told
myself disconsolately: "They'll already be yellow and
wrinkled and I haven't eaten a one." Because, that same
night, Mauricia began to find herself unwell, and no
longer could get up from bed, and she insisted on writing
to grandmother (oh, why, why had it happened?). I
tried to bring the little cart of my memories toward the
golden twigs in the orchard, or to the greenish-toned
branches, glowing in the bottom of the puddles. (I
thought about one puddle, in particular, over which
green mosquitoes swarmed, and next to which I stood
listening as they looked for me, without answering their
calls, because it was the day grandmother came to fetch
me—I saw the dust that was raised by the car on the
distant highway—to take me with her to the island.)
And I remembered the chestnut-colored stains of the islands on the pale blue of my maps (dearest atlas!).
Suddenly, the bed and its twisted shadows on the wall,
toward which the ants crawled, suddenly—I said to myself—the bed was nailed on the yellow and green island,
surrounded on all sides by a dull blue. And the forged-
iron shadow, behind my head—the bed was almost a
handbreadth from the wall—gave me a sensation of great
insecurity. Fortunately, I carried with me, hidden between my sweater and my chest, my black boy rag doll—
Gorogó, Chimney Sweep—and now I had it there, under
my pillow. Then, I realized I had lost something: for-

gotten in the mountains, in the enormous and shabby house: my tiny cardboard theater. (I closed my eyes and saw the transparent paper decorations, with blue, pink, and yellow skies and windows, and those black letters on the back: *Children's Theater, Seix y Barral, cable address: Arapil. First frame, Number 3 . . . "The Star of the Three Wise Men," "The Soul of the Ruins,"* and the enormous and prosaic mystery of the small transparent windows. Oh, how I desired once more to be there, to cross the pieces of paper, and flee through their false caramel windows. Ah, yes, and my albums and books: *Kay and Gerda, in Their Garden above the Rooftops, The Little Mermaid Embracing the Statue, The Eleven Swan Princes.* And I felt a blind rage against myself. And against grandmother, because no one reminded me of that, and I no longer had it. Lost, lost, just like the green grasshoppers, like the October apples, like the wind in the black chimney. And, above all, I could not even remember in what closet I stored the theater; only Mauricia knew it.) I did not sleep, and I saw the dawn for the first time in my life, through the slats of the shutters.

Grandmother took me to the village, to her house. What a great surprise when I awoke with the sun, and went, barefoot, with a warm dream still hanging on my eyelids, toward the window. There were striped blue and white curtains, and further below, the Descent. (Golden days, unmatched, the veil of the sun caught among the black trunks of the almond trees below, rushing toward the sea.) The Descent was a revelation. I could not have suspected it behind the house and walls of the neglected garden with its dark cherry trees and silvery-armed fig tree. I probably did not realize it then, but at the sudden view of the Descent I must have had a sharp presentiment of great happiness and grief. Then, they took me again to the city, and placed me as a boarder in Our Lady of the Angels. Without knowing why or how, I felt malevolent and rebellious there; as if they had stuck a small piece of glass in my heart, as had happened, one morning, to tiny Kay. And I felt an enormous pleasure in that, and in hiding (together with my memories and vague, confused love for a lost time) all that might have shown weakness, or at least, what seemed to me weakness. I never cried.

During the first vacations I played with Borja very little. My untamed and sullen nature was ascribed to my country background, and everyone was assured my character would change. A year and a half later, as spring came—I was just fourteen—they expelled me, amid great scandal and consternation, from Our Lady of the Angels.

In grandmother's house, there was coldness and promises of great corrections. But for the first time I won, if not the sympathy, the hidden admiration of Borja, who allowed me to enter his company and confidences.

Right in the middle of vacation, war broke out. Aunt Emilia and Borja were not able to return to the peninsula, and Uncle Álvaro, who was a colonel, was at the front. Borja and I, startled, like victims of some strange ambush, understood that we would have to stay on the island for an indefinite period of time. Our respective schools remained distant, and the atmosphere was shot through with something exciting that influenced the adults—grandmother, Aunt Emilia, the village priest, the doctor—and lent an air of abnormality to their dreary lives. The times were out of joint: long-respected customs were broken. At any given moment or hour, visits and messages arrived. Antonia came and went with bits of news. The radio, old and noisy, previously forgotten and despised by grandmother, came to be something magical and ferocious which at night focused the attention and united in a rare complicity those who once treated each other ceremoniously. My grandmother pressed her large head to the hulking contraption, and, if the coveted voice disappeared, she shook it frantically, as if in this way she might return the wave length to its listening point. Perhaps all this was what made the relationship, cold up until then, more intimate between Borja and me.

The calm, the silence, and a long and exasperating wait, in which, of a sudden, we could see ourselves all submerged, also worked on us. We were bored and disquieted alternately, as if full of a slow and watchful worry, ready to leap at any moment. I began to know the house, spacious and strange, with its ocher-colored walls and clay roof, its long loggia with stone balustrade and wooden ceiling, where Borja and I, our faces toward the floor, carried on whispered conversations. (Our whispering must have had a chilling echo above, in the caissoned niches, as if our voices were stolen away and transported by tiny beings from beam to beam, from nook to nook.) Borja and I, stretched across the floor, feigned a game of chess on the worn-out ivory chessboard which had belonged to our grandfather. At times, Borja screamed out a pretentious *Au roi!* (because grandmother and Aunt Emilia liked us to practice our detestable French with its island accent). In this way, the two of us found in the loggia—where my grandmother did not like to walk, and which she could only see through the open windows—the unique refuge in that maddening house, always echoing the heavy footsteps of grandmother, who, like a whippet, somehow got wind of our flights to the village, the Descent, the cove of Santa Catalina, the Port . . . To escape, we would take off our shoes so that she might not hear our steps. But suddenly the witch would discover our elongated shadows crossing the floor. With her low, swinish gaze, she would see us flee (as she could see, perhaps, her turbid life flee within herself), and she would let her cane and her snuff box fall (her whole bosom spotted) and then she would howl:

"Borja!"

Borja, the hypocrite, quickly put on his shoes, his leg bent like a crane (I can still see him smiling on one side, biting the corner of his mouth, his lips glistening like those of a loose woman; at times he actually seemed a loose woman, and not a young fellow of fifteen with fuzz already under his nose).

"Too late, the beast has seen us . . ."

(As soon as we were alone, we competed to see who could use the worse language.) Borja would emerge slowly, wearing an innocent air, as grandmother came up, hitting the furniture here and there with her little cane, clumsy as a rhinoceros in water, panting, her white anger over her forehead, and said:

"Where were you going . . . without Lauro?"

"We were going to the Descent for a little while . . ."

(Here I am now, facing this terribly green glass, my heart heavy. Is it true that life stems from scenes like this? Is it true that as children we lived our entire life, in one gulp, only to repeat ourselves stupidly, blindly, without any sense, forever afterwards?)

Borja did not have any affection for me, but he needed me and he preferred to have me within his hoop, as he had Lauro. Lauro was the son of Antonia, grandmother's housekeeper. Antonia was the same age as grandmother, whom she had served since childhood. When she became a widow, with Lauro still very small (grandmother had married off Antonia at her own convenience), grandmother again took her into the house, and they sent the boy first to the Monastery, where he sang in the choir and dressed in a skirt, and then to the Seminary. (*Lauro the Chink. Lauro the Chink.* He sometimes said: "This is an old and wicked island. An island of Phoenicians and merchants, leeches and fakes: oh, greedy merchants! In the houses of this village, in the outside walls and secret inside walls, in every place, there are golden coins buried." (I imagined liquid treasures, mixed with the glowing bones of the dead, under the ground, among the roots of the woods. The golden coins were like luminous, burning coals scattered among stones and worms in the monasteries.) And if Lauro spoke—as he usually did—at night on the Descent, the three of us were united by his mysterious words, carried away by his soft voice, and I, at times, would close my eyes. Perhaps those were the only good moments we allowed him. In the darkness, fireflies wandered, like miniature floating boats, the same as those that sailed over the Little Mermaid and made her shudder with nostalgia. (Boats of red silk and bamboo, sailed by the strange, black-eyed boy who was not able to give her a soul.) The Chink would suddenly fall silent and wipe his forehead with his handkerchief. It was apparent that when he spoke about the merchants he allowed himself the only fury permitted to a servant permanently bent low. Borja would become impatient: "Go on, Chink." Lauro would clean his green glass lenses, and when he took them off, the wide eyelids of his Mongolian eyes appeared half-closed. "I'm tired, Master Borja . . . the damp air brings out my hoarseness . . . I . . ." "Don't stop!" And Borja would press his hand against Lauro's chest as if to push him. The Chink stared at Borja's hand, its fingers open like five tiny daggers. "Let me go up to sleep . . . I'm very sad, let me go . . . What do you know about these things? Have you lost something, perhaps? You've never lost anything!" As we did not understand, Borja laughed. (I was thinking: "Have I lost something? I don't know: I only know I haven't found anything." And it was as if someone or something might have betrayed me at some unknown time.) We were not good to him. "Mr.

Preceptor, Mr. Chink . . ." We called him Prespective, Prespective Raven, Yellow Judas . . . and whatever other stupid name came into our heads, under the twining of cherry branches or the fig tree on which the stubborn cock of Son Major used to climb. (Why do I now remember the cock of Son Major? It was a virile and valiant cock with irritable eyes that glistened in the sun. It escaped from Son Major to come and climb onto the fig tree in our garden.)

Lauro had spent many years in the Seminary, but, in the end, he could not be a priest. Grandmother, who paid for his studies, was not pleased. For the moment, he became our teacher and companion. At times, looking at him, I thought perhaps something had occurred in the Seminary similar to what happened to me in Our Lady of the Angels.

"Rejected priest," we said to him. I imitated Borja in everything.

The rejected priest had sad, Mongolian eyes, and a silky, black, scarcely-born beard. The yellow, round pupils of his eyes were difficult to make out behind the green crystals of his glasses: *The Chink*.

"For goodness' sake, heavens, don't call me that in front of your grandmother! Maintain your dignity, please, or she'll put me in the street . . ."

The Chink looked at Borja, his lips trembling over his protruding, widely spaced teeth.

Borja, with the knife he had taken away from Guiem, cut away at a stick. He laughed to himself and threw the green, moist, beautifully perfumed wood in the air.

The pieces of wood fell to the ground of the garden, just beyond the Chink's head. Borja put his open hand to his ear:

"What are you saying, what are you saying? I don't hear well: look inside my ears, I have something buzzing there. I don't know if it's a bee . . ."

The flattened cheekbones of the Chink blushed a rosy hue. *In front of grandmother, no.* (But in front of grandmother, Borja appeared self-confident, good.) Borja would kiss grandmother's hand and his mother's. Borja would cross himself, his rosary bead between his golden fingers, like a little friar. That is what he seemed to be, with bare chestnut-colored feet in sandals. And he would say:

"Mysteries of Sorrow . . ."

(Borja, the great faker, and yet, how pure we were still.)

I remember a warm low wind, a sky swollen like a grey infection, the pale prickly pears, scarcely green, and the land all spreading down from a height, from the crests of mountains where the oak and beech woods were inhabited by charcoal burners, to open out onto a valley, with its village, and then run down the Descent, behind our house, to the sea. And I remember the coppery earth of the Descent graded downward by the staggered steps of retaining walls: the whitewashed stones like enormous sets of teeth, one on top of another, looming over the sea undulating there below.

Suddenly, the wind stopped, and Borja, in the study

room with me and the Chink, lifted his head and listened, as if he had heard something mysterious and important. (On the floor above, in her boudoir, grandmother was tearing off the wrapper from the recently received newspapers with her greedy paws. Her fingers trembled avidly, the diamonds turned toward the palm of her hand. Grandmother searched and scoured the papers for news of the *red hydra* and its excesses; for photographs of noble priests rent open from top to bottom.)

I remember: perhaps it was five in the afternoon that particular day, when the wind had suddenly dropped. Borja's profile was thin as the cutting edge of a dagger. He raised his upper lip in a special way, and his eye-teeth, long and sharp, like the whitest of peeled pine nuts, gave him a fierce air.

"Shut up now, you old crane," he said.

Halfway through a passage in Cicero, the Chink blinked, confused. And he begged, immediately:

"Borja . . ." interrupting himself.

He looked over his green glasses, through the yellow haze of his eyes, and once again, and again, I asked myself why he so feared a brat of fifteen. Borja also had me in his clutches, true enough, though it was not clear how. If some night I awoke thirsty, and, half-asleep, lit the lamp on the night table and looked for the glass covered with a starched cloth (Antonia ritually put one in all the rooms every night), I knew, as I wet my lips in the fresh water, that I had been dreaming Borja held me down with a chain and dragged me behind him, like some fantastic puppeteer. I would rebel and want to scream—as when I was small, in the country—but Borja would hold me by force. (And why, why, if I still had not committed any serious error, why and how could he intimidate me with the secret?)

Seated at one end of the table, he twirled a yellow pencil. The balcony doors were open and a piece of brilliant grey sky could be seen. Borja went outside and I got up to follow him. Lauro the Chink looked at me, and I saw obvious hatred in his eyes, a hatred so thick it could almost be touched in the air. I laughed at him as I had learned from Borja:

"What's the matter, you old monkey?"

He was not old, he was scarcely past twenty, but he seemed ageless, sunk into himself, as if eating himself up alive. (Borja said he had heard him whipping himself, on his knees: he had peered through the lock of Lauro's wretched attic room, on whose walls hung religious prints and reproductions of the stained-glass window of a cathedral in some town or other, placed around a tiny brown saint that looked like Borja with his curly hair and bare feet. And there was also a photograph of his mother and him, hand in hand: the boy in his seminarian's skirt, his stockings sagging.) But Lauro the Chink was not afraid of me as he was of Borja:

"Miss Matia, you stay here."

Borja came back. His skin was glowing and he made the pencil roll between his fingers. He half closed his eyes:

"Latin is finished, Mr. Prespective . . ."

Lauro the Chink put his long yellow finger to his temple. He murmured something between his thick lips, which showed the row of widely spaced teeth.

"Where are you going? Your grandmother will ask about you . . ."

Borja threw the pencil on the table and it rolled with a slight rattle on its trapezoid sides.

"Your grandmother will say: 'Where are the children, Lauro? How is it you've left them alone?' And I, what am I going to answer? She doesn't like to see you wandering around . . ."

Borja threw his arms back, swung them like pendulums, and then raised them, so he could hang from the doorjamb of the balcony. He contracted his legs like a young rabbit, his knees raised, brilliant in the pallid light. He swung like a monkey. To be sure, there was something apelike in Borja, as in all my family on the maternal side. He laughed:

"Borja, Borja . . ."

The wind, as I said, had stopped. Before presenting himself to grandmother, Borja first dressed in blue denim pants, worn out in the seat and tight over the thighs, and an old brown sweater, stretched on all sides. His neck emerged thin and firm from the round neckline, and he seemed even more like an apocryphal friar.

"Borja, Master Borja: if your father, the colonel, should come one day . . ."

His father, the colonel: I covered my lips with my hand to pretend a laughing fit. His father, the colonel, would not come, perhaps he never would come. (Aunt

Emilia, with her wide, velvet-white jaws and her small, pinky eyes, would remain waiting, waiting, waiting, will-lessly, with her prominent breasts and her big soft stomach. There was something obscene in everything about her, in her waiting, in her looking toward the window.)

We were like this for more than a month, with no change. "When the war is over . . ." "The war will be a matter of days," they said, but it turned out rather differently there on the island. Grandmother scrutinized the sea with her opera glasses, which she wiped with the point of her handkerchief, and there was nothing, nothing. A couple of times, enemy planes passed high overhead. However, there *was* something, like an enormous evil under the earth, under the stones, the rooftops, the skulls. When the siesta hour came to the village, or else when a shadow of quiet fell, in those expectant moments, the footsteps of the Taronjí brothers resounded in the narrow streets. The Taronjís: with their high boots, their tight military jackets half buttoned up, blond and pale, with round blue eyes like those of monstrous babies, and their large Judaic noses. (Ah, the Taronjís: the island, the village, the somber charcoal burners, scarcely dared to look at them above ankle-level, when they passed by.) The Taronjís took the suspects to the ditch beside the road, where the woods began, beyond the plaza of the Jews; or to the place on the way back from the cliff after passing Son Major.

"Borja, Borja . . ."

Borja continued swinging himself, as long as he could.

Then he let himself go and fell to the ground, rubbing his wrists and looking at us from under his thick golden eyelids, like sections of tangerine.

"You idiotic ape," he said. "If Papa comes, I'll tell him everything, everything . . . You'd better pray for him not to come, even if you can't pray because you don't believe in anything . . . I'll tell Papa and he'll turn you over to the Taronjís . . . Do you know what happens to old perverted apes like you?"

The Chink bit his lips. Borja came closer to the table again, scratching an arm:

"It's calmed down now, girl," he said, "shall we go?"

"She hasn't finished her translation . . . Not her," meowed Lauro the Chink, poor teacher of the young Borja and Matia.

(Poor, poor monkey with his nocturnal laments and his moist glance, grandmother's protégé, with his tied, twisted, packaged hatred, like a bundle of dirty clothes abandoned under the bed. Poor Lauro the Chink, sad teacher without any youth, without any shared ribaldry, with memorized words and the heart of a mole. His hands were those of a frustrated farmer, the edges of his fingers yellowed and his nails bitten.) Something had given me a presentiment of the secret between Borja and the Chink, but even though Borja spoke to me of those things at times, I still did not understand them. (Once the Chink took us to his lair in the attic, where he used to scorch through the siesta hour, under the tiles of the roof that burned in the sun like an oven. And there, he took off his little black jacket for the first time, and his sweaty armpits became visible. He rolled up his sleeves, and his arms were covered with soft black hair. Then he took off his necktie and loosened his collar. Borja jumped on his rickety old bed, which began to groan as if alarmed by his weight, and the dust blew out of the cracks. (The whole house was full of dust.) In that attic room there were traces of love, the love of Antonia, his mother. Antonia was in the flowers which bordered the window and which the sun seemed to set afire. They were—how well I remember them!—a burning red in the form of a chalice, and they had something violent about them, like the hatred locked up in Lauro. And there, in the mirror, stuck in the frame, was the photograph: he and his mother with his arm around her shoulders. He, an ugly child with his hair in swirls and his stockings sagging under his seminarian's habit. His mother went up to the attic every day and dusted the thousand trifles: painting reproductions, clay figures, flowers, shells. If grandmother had known that we went up there, she would have let out a howl. The Chink put his arms around our shoulders and brought us closer to the mirror. I sensed on my bare back—it was so hot that we did not dress as grandmother ordered until lunchtime, when we presented ourselves for the first time in front of her—his hand going up and down, just like the rats over the cornices of the roof, and though I did not say anything, it filled me with anxiety. Lauro caressed Borja and me at the same time, and said:

"Two such creatures, good God, from another world . . ."

At last, as if coming out of an enchantment, Borja freed us from the Chink's grasp.)

"The wind has died down," Borja repeated, looking at me.

Lauro the Chink decided to smile. He closed the book, from which a weak cloud of dust puffed—the sun began to open a passage through the moist warm fog—and he said, with false optimism:

"Good, we'll go, then . . ."

"You're not coming."

Lauro the Chink took out his handkerchief and wiped his forehead slowly. Then he brought it for a moment under his nose and pressed it against his upper lip, tapping himself with little weak blows. Afterwards he dried his neck, between his shirt and his skin.

Borja and I went out to the Descent.

2

We always left through the back door. We stuck close to the wall, until we disappeared from grandmother's field of vision; she thought we were in class. From the window of her boudoir, she scrutinized her row of tiny white square houses, where the tenant farmers lived. Those houses, at sundown, glowed with yellowish lights, and were like pawns in a toy world, and their inhabitants, dolls. Seated in her rocking chair or in the black leather chair with gilt nails, grandmother focused her opera glasses of yellowish satin incrusted with their false sapphires, and played at looking. Between the dark trunks of the almonds and the leaves of the olive trees the Descent ran down toward the rocks of the coast.

Borja's boat was called *Leontina*. Some steps carved in the rock gave access to the small pier. Only the two of us used to go there. In the *Leontina,* we skirted the rocky coast, up to the small cove of Santa Catalina. There was not another cove for several kilometers, and we called it the cemetery of boats because the mariners of the Port abandoned their unserviceable craft there.

It was very hot and Borja skipped in front of me. To go to Santa Catalina, the best way was by sea. By land it proved to be dangerous: the high, rough rocks cut like knives. Between the last of the tree trunks, the sea glimmered a pale green, as lifeless as a sheet of metal.

"And the others?"

"Bah, they won't come."

I was thinking of the Guiems who were always against Borja. On Borja's side were the sons of the administrator and Juan Antonio, the doctor's son. It was perpetual war. But Santa Catalina belonged only to Borja and myself. We jumped aboard the *Leontina* which rocked and creaked. In its time it had been painted green and white, but now its color was indeterminate. Borja took up the oars, and pressing his foot against a rock he gave a push. The boat moved smoothly out to the open sea.

The beach at Santa Catalina was very small and at the edge of the water it was fringed with golden shells which crumbled under our feet when we jumped from the boat, as if we were crushing pieces of crockery. Out of the hard sand, in which footsteps scarcely left an imprint, grew pitas and green reeds. It always seemed to me that there was something fateful about the cove, as if it were being shaken by a catastrophic wind. There, disemboweled, their corroded ribs sticking up into the air, old friends of ours already, lay the *Young Simón* and the *Margelida*, their names half-erased from their sides. No one any longer knew what the others had been called. From the center of the *Young Simón* sprung a tall clump of reeds, like a strange green sail. And a cable still wound around the tackle, staining the rushes with rust.

Inside the *Young Simón* Borja kept the carbine, and the iron box containing his treasures: the money we stole from grandmother and Aunt Emilia, the deck of cards, cigarettes, a flashlight, and some other mysterious packages of his, all wrapped in an old black raincoat. At the bottom of the hatchway were stored the bottles of brandy we took from grandfather's room, and another bottle of a sweetish, sticky liquor Borja had discovered where it had been forgotten in the kitchen, and which, in reality, we did not like. All these stores had disappeared, little by little, from grandfather's black wardrobe, thanks to a small skeleton key which Guiem —son of a blacksmith—made for Borja during one of the truces between the two gangs. There were periods when Guiem's gang and Borja's gang got along, and they exchanged Borja's invaluable possessions (Borja alone kept the tiny iron key for the box, and it hung from the same chain as his medal) for Guiem's dark utensils: knives and skeleton keys. There was also a contrivance—two rusty iron hooks—for the carbine, wrapped lovingly in greasy rags, bandaged and covered with oint- ment like an Egyptian mummy. The bullets he kept in his bedroom. Everything came from the same place: Borja was a ferret, a real vulture when it came to our dead grandfather's things. The three rooms that had be- longed to grandfather exercised a tremendous attraction on Borja and me. It was a strange, luxurious-monastic suite, like everything in grandmother's house: an odd mixture of valuable objects, filth, clumsy furniture of heavy wood, fine porcelains, and a gold table service—a gift from the king to our great-grandfather—weapons, rust, cobwebs, and a minimum of cleanliness. (I shall always remember the old chipped bathtub, with its patches of black, and Antonia, her head turned to one side and her eyes closed, holding out the towel with which to dry us, rubbing as if she wanted to turn us in- side out.) Borja could enter grandfather's locked rooms (there was a vague and unconfessed superstition, as if that cruel man's soul floated through his three adjoining rooms, which kept us at bay) by clambering over one end of the loggia's balustrade. Then he crawled along the cornices until he reached the window, with its broken pane, which reflected the brilliance of the low sun, like an anticipation of hell; then he opened the latch through the hole in the window. He plunged into the green and humid obscurity of time piled on time, among the lami- nated butterflies and the cadaver of a bat—yes, of a dead bat turned to ash behind the bookcase. In his searches he found that book of the Jews, the one which described

how they burned the Jews in the little plaza in the outskirts, next to the oak grove. The words of the book ran
down my spine like a damp rat, when in the boat or the
shadows of the dim study room, with its balcony open
to the Descent, (or some night on the loggia, our meeting place when everybody was in bed, and after we had
silently jumped through the windows of our rooms in
our bare feet) Borja would read it to me, savoring every
word, so as to terrorize me. We had the entire day to
ourselves, but only at night, smoking a forbidden cigarette and without clearly seeing one another's face, did
we make confessions we would never have listened to
nor made in the light of day. And what we said on the
loggia at night we would never repeat the following day,
as if we had forgotten it.

The deck of cards and the bottles, our booty, lay
wrapped in an old raincoat aboard the *Young Simón*.
(Poor Lauro the Chink. Borja also kept there the
wretched and humiliating proof of Lauro's guilt, in his
own handwriting, amid the odor of rotting fish still sticking to the planks of the *Young Simón*.) Many times he
went there alone because he liked to lie on the deck of
the boat, belly upwards, under the sun. He said the sun
did him a lot of good, and, consequently, he was very
tanned: bronze or gold, depending on the quality of the
light or shade inside the house. How true it was—Borja,
Borja—that if we were not able to love each other as
brother and sister, as the Holy Mother Church com-
mands, at least we kept each other company. (Perhaps,
I think now, with all your blarney, with your proud

hardheartedness, my poor brother, were you not perhaps as solitary an animal as myself, as almost all the children in the world?) At that time, beneath the red silence of the sun, behind the criminals' faces—the Taronjís, the photographs that came from beyond the sea—and the selfish or indifferent old men, as rotted out as the Santa Catalina boats, we did not dare confess to our sadness. And the shadow of your father—"the colonel"—always present, along with grandmother's newspapers, with their horrendous photographs—pastiche? reality? What difference did it make!—of men rent open, hanging from hooks like beasts, from doorjambs. (And shots in the outskirts, down the road, at the edge of the cliff, beyond Son Major. A scream perhaps, fearfully sounding one afternoon, as we were hidden among the olive trees of the Descent.)

Borja taught us how to play cards. Neither I, nor the sons of the administrator, nor Juan Antonio, the doctor's son—we serfs, Borja's personal property—had ever before seen the queen of spades or hearts, and we would lose our weekly allowance, our savings, and money that was not ours. But we went on playing. Even Guiem, stubborn and dull, stupid and cunning, with his big rabbinical nose, managed to catch on to a royal flush. It was the only thing Aunt Emilia, Borja's mother, had ever taught him.

That afternoon the little beach seemed on fire. There was a pulsation of light in the air or perhaps within us. It was impossible to tell.

We had scarcely stepped on the sand when Borja stopped:

"Be quiet," he said.

Our legs were still wet. The grains of sand glistened like particles of tin around Borja's ankles.

The man was face down, with an arm stretched out on the ground, close to the belly of the boat, like a dog looking for a place to sleep. He must have fallen and rolled down toward the sea, until he ended up against the *Young Simón*. Nearby, behind the rocks, a gull began to screech. Among the broken-bottomed boats, worn by the wind, the shadows stretched out aslant.

The sand gave off a sweetish vapor which clung to the skin. Through the swollen, smoke-colored clouds, the red balloon of the sun intensified minute by minute, like an ulcer. Borja murmured:

"He's dead . . ."

Behind the boat, first a shadow appeared, and then a boy. I thought I had seen him at some time before, perhaps in the orchard of his house, and just then I was sure he was not a stranger to me. He was, I thought, one of Malene's family, who had a small house and orchard on the Descent. They lived, between their walls, as on a lost island in the middle of grandmother's land, quite close to the sea. Some small holdings they once had beyond the Descent had been confiscated. They were a segregated, marked group. There was another family in the village like them, but Malene's was the most harassed, perhaps because they were cousins of the Taronjís and because there existed between them a long-standing

and vast hatred. These things we knew through Antonia.
The hatred, I will remember, nourished the life of the
village like a great root, and the Taronjí brothers proclaimed it from one side to another: from the olive groves
to the back side of the mountain, and even as far away
as the high oak thickets where the charcoal burners lived.
The Taronjís and Malene's husband had the same name,
they were relatives, but they could not have detested one
another more. The hatred burst out in the middle of the
silence, like the sun, like a bloodshot and bleeding eye
through the haze. On the island the sun always seemed
sinister to me. It polished the stones of the plaza and left
them brilliant and slippery like bones or like an evil and
rare ivory. They were the same stones where the footsteps of the Taronjí brothers resounded; and the Taronjís
were relatives of José Taronjí, father of that boy who
came out from behind the boat, and whose name, suddenly, came to me: Manuel. Without knowing why, I
said to myself: "Something has happened, and the
Taronjís are to blame." (Them, always them. Their feet
treading, with a special echo, the paving stones of the
streets or the ruins of the old part of town, which had
burned down many years ago and where only the plaza
of the Jews remained, next to the woods. Burnt walls, big,
blackened and mysterious hollows, in which doors were
cut to be used for storing feed and wood.) In the tiny
plaza of the Jews we sometimes found ourselves with
the "others." Seeing that boy, I thought vividly about
them, about Guiem and company: Guiem, Toni from
Abrés, Antonio of Son Lluch, Ramón and Sebastián.

Guiem was older than all the others: sixteen. Toni, fifteen; Antonio, fifteen; Ramón, thirteen—he was tolerated because he was more malicious than anyone else. And Sebastián the Cripple, fourteen years and eight months. (He always said fifteen.) But this boy, Manuel, was not part of either group. (Once again, I recalled him, I knew him: his back, bent over the earth, right there on the Descent. The door of the orchard, burned by the sea air, was open. And I remembered him with his face to the stony ground, which bore flowers and vegetables, over the small, damp, and sandy parcel of earth. Suddenly, the flowers, quiet as the earth, red and alive, curved like a skin, like a quivering of sun, screaming in the midst of the silence. And there was a well between the pitas, with a grey sun licking the rusty chain. Within the walls grew the exultant greenness, the fresh and compact leaves of the vegetables from which the family nourished themselves. It was, I told myself confusedly, like feeding oneself on some hidden anger in the heart of the earth. He was bent over, and he belonged to no one. No one wanted to help them harvest the olives, or the almonds from their few trees. The Taronjís carried off the father; and now Malene the mother, Manuel, and the two younger children, María and Bartolomé, did the work. Their house was small, square, and without a tiled roof: a white and simple cube, and in the doorway, behind the white-washed columns of the porch, a striped blue curtain was puffed out by the wind. They had a dog that howled at the moon, at the sea, at everything, and showed its teeth since the day the Taronjís carried off José, the father, at dawn. They were like another island, right in the middle of my grandmother's land; an island with its house, its well, the vegetables from which they fed themselves, and the purple, yellow, and black flowers, where the mosquitoes and bees buzzed, and the light seemed made of honey. I saw Manuel bent over the earth, barefoot, but Manuel was no peasant. His father, José, had been the administrator for the master of Son Major, and then he married Malene. The villagers took a dim view of Malene—Antonia would say—and the master of Son Major made them a gift of the house and land.) And then again, without understanding how or why, and as quickly as a single breath, I remembered Antonia telling grandmother: "José Taronjí had the lists." Grandmother listened to her while two golden butterflies fastened themselves avidly to the tube of the crystal lamp; they died trembling and fell to the floor like bits of ash. Lauro explained it in greater detail: "They had it all very well organized: they divided Son Major and he distributed it very well: who was going to live on the ground floor, who on the floor above . . . And this, your house also, Doña Práxedes . . ." It was the same voice he used when he said: "They've sprayed a village in Extremadura with gasoline and burned alive two seminarians who had hidden in a haystack. They burned them alive, the damnable wretches . . . They are killing all the decent people, they are filling the country with Martyrs, and more Martyrs . . ." (The Chink and the Martyrs, the stained-glass windows of Santa María with their dead brothers on high, and behind it all, the evil and ferocious sun brilliantly driving through the ruby-red, the emerald, the warm, goldenish yellow. And the Chink going on like a sleepwalker: "We'll have altars covered with blood and in new stained-glass windows we'll see the faces of so many, many brothers of ours . . .")

It was Manuel's father who was carried off by the Taronjís, who wore high riding boots and never rode on horseback. Manuel left the convent where he lived, and for the time being was there, in the orchard, working for them because no one in the village helped them. And another time I remember the Chink's voice saying: "Like before, when the lepers went to David's door ringing bells so that the uncontaminated might leave, that's the way they should be forced to announce themselves as they go about with their pestilential ideas . . ."

It was Manuel, the young boy, who came out from behind the boat, no doubt of it; that was his back bent over the earth we had seen beyond the door corroded by sea air; it was the nape of his dark neck, the harsh color of sun over sweat, not the smooth goldness of Borja. And the sun was also in the color of his burnt hair, dried by the sun's fire, in coppery fringes. "A redhead like all of them," Borja finally said. "A redhead. A dirty *Chueta,* a Jew."

3

I could not tell if he was crying, because his face was covered with sweat.

"Lend me the boat," he said.

I thought the rage of the flowers would throb in his voice, but it was an opaque voice, without nuances. As I faced him, it seemed to me I had never seen him before. His face was not as dark as the back of his neck. I hardly remember his features, only his eyes, black and flashing, with their prominent corneas, almost blue. His eyes were unlike those of anyone else. He was tall and well-built for his age. Just looking at him, I thought he hardly needed to ask Borja for the boat: he could have taken it simply by stepping forward and giving my cousin a push. Borja's bare legs and long-toed feet, with a nail broken on the big toe of his right foot, were still damp and covered with sand. They seemed totally helpless next to the massive figure of Manuel. And Manuel, suddenly, was not a boy. No, it was certainly true (perhaps from the very moment in which he had asked for the boat, in the cove of Santa Catalina, with a gull overhead shrieking inharmoniously and inopportunely) that his infancy, his youth, and even life itself seemed very distant. And surely, he could not have been sixteen yet.

The body of the man was still stuck like a barnacle to the keel of the *Young Simón*. I do not remember if we were scared. It is only now, perhaps, that I feel fear like a breath upon me, remembering how he spoke to us. I can still see the reeds, so tender, sprouting from the sand, and the violent blue of the pitas. One was broken, with its edges dried up like a scar.

At first I thought those were tears glistening on his cheeks. But he was covered with sweat and I could not be sure. I thought: "How did he get here without a boat?" He must have come down across the rocks. In spite of the sweetish heat that seemed to emanate from both earth and sky, I felt cold. "They have thrown the man down from up there, down to the rocks." Something began to shine. Perhaps it was the earth. Suddenly everything was tremendously brilliant. I raised my head and saw how the sun, at last, was tearing a rent in the clouds. Its red and furious authority over the sand and water was palpable. The gull stopped shrieking and in that great silence (it was suddenly like a mute thunderclap rolling over us) I told myself: "That man is dead, they've killed him. He's dead."

(The Taronjís, Lauro the Chink, Antonia . . . And also Lorenza, the cook, and Ton, her husband. It was some days ago now: "They've put the five of them in the corral. The two Taronjís climbed the wall and their own men pointed their pistols at them. And they couldn't talk, struck dumb." It was not sweat but tears that Lorenza shed, listening to her husband tell about it. They did not know I had gone to fetch the ropes and bring them to Borja where he waited for me. I hid behind the kitchen, beside the patio. They spoke in their own language, but I understood them. I climbed the short ladder to the storeroom. It smelled strongly of the ashes used for making soap and of the almond shells piled up on the other side. I pushed my finger through the broken glass, dull and grey with dust and sticky dirt. I could see her seated, with the knife between her hands: the only thing that gleamed. Her eyes were lowered and glistening drops fell downward. I held my breath, listening to the voice of her husband, Ton. I could only see his shadow, which came and went over the red bricks of the floor, I could only hear the noise of his hissed *s*'s; he was speaking in a low voice. "And the wife of the administrator said: 'And that one, reading *El Liberal* every day? And never setting foot in church.' And Taronjí hit him with the butt of his gun. Meanwhile, the others wanted to push open the door. I tell you, woman, they were like animals; yes, just like animals. They tied the charcoal burners' hands behind their backs, and the poor fellows looked up in a way that was awful. Then the older Taronjí said: 'Open it!' And then they took them out. Riera's son climbed into the car, you know which one, that black car they have from the Town Hall, and they started off. The older Taronjí looked at me and said: 'Better go home, Ton. Better if you don't see any of these things.' He knows she'll defend me, after all. Don't you think she'll defend me? They've always paid attention to her. Don't you think so?" By his tone, I understood that "she" was my grandmother, who would have to defend Ton from the Taronjís or from someone. But —I said to myself—nothing or no one mattered to grandmother. And then Lorenza saw me, because the stair creaked. She was really frightened, and said: "Good God, what are you doing there, what are you doing there?" And she looked at me in a strange way and it seemed to me that her lips were drained of color, and she used the polite form of address, in spite of the fact that when she was not in front of grandmother she never did. And I saw that her face was drawn and her eyes dry. It seemed strange that she should have cried at all. Her husband, Ton, disappeared at once: I heard his steps going toward the patio, as if he were running away. I got down off the ladder and felt the inside of my mouth turning bitter from some seed I had put in it.)

It was true: the fallen man, stuck to the *Young Simón*, was dead.

"Who is he?" asked Borja, in a hoarse voice. And Manuel answered:

"My father."

I turned my back. I was surprised. I had heard many things and caught glimpses of photographs in newspapers, but this was real. There was a dead man, thrown over the precipice into the cove.

"He wanted to escape when they carried him off . . ."

It did not seem true, it seemed unlikely, something from out of a nightmare. But it was Manuel, his son, who was saying it. And he was there, in front of us, with his shadow growing longer on the earth, slanted and unreal. One could see the trembling of his legs, firmly planted, yet he spoke slowly, measuring his words, in a lusterless voice. And it was sweat, only sweat, that fell from his cheeks. A very shiny drop rolled down the side of his nose to his mouth, and it was also sweat. Not one, not one single tear. And he went on, his lips white, tilting his hand, indicating the trajectory of the body to its landing place still marked in the sand.

"Let me have the boat," he repeated. "I want to take him home."

Borja backed up toward the rocks. The gull started to shriek again. We sat down very close together, so close our knees touched, next to a prickly pear plant. Borja was very pale, he wrapped his arms around his knees, and with his head bent over he looked across the wide leaves of the plant. I imitated him. I looked for his hand and he held mine a moment, pressing it hard. His almond eyes were inundated with sunlight, as if emptied; and in them there was also an overwhelming stupefaction. He said:

"I suppose by letting him have it we aren't doing anything bad . . ."

Manuel turned the man face upwards, and we saw part of the sand stained dark red.

"How long could he have been there?" my cousin said very quietly.

Manuel dragged him toward the edge of the sea. The man was not wearing socks, and his bare ankles showed under the edge of his pants. His shoes were brand new, as if he might have put on his Sunday clothes.

"Yes, it's true," added Borja, looking against his will, and to one side, through the hollows of the prickly pear, "Yes, it is José, his father. Damn him, taking off like this in my boat . . ."

And he added:

"Listen, you, not a word to anyone."

I assented with my head. At that moment, Manuel crossed the fringe of shells, which shone in the bright

sun like an immovable wave of fire. The body dragged
the shells and buried them with its weight, with a muffled clinking sound. All of a sudden Borja yelled out:

"Hurry up! Or do you want my grandmother to find
out?"

Manuel did not answer. The trembling of his legs
could be seen between the green leaves covered with
thorns. He had stained the sides of his shirt with blood,
as if he had tried to carry the man on his shoulders and
had not been able to support his weight. He dragged him
like a sack. There was nothing else to do.

Then: the splash of water and the noise of a body falling to the bottom of the boat. It was a dull thud, as if
muffled by rags. It was obviously a dead body being
dropped in the boat. I stood up and looked across the
prickly pear. Manuel, with the oar, pushed the boat
away from the rocks. Then he stayed there, poised in the
prow, aiming the oar at us for a second, as if it were
a weapon, while the *Leontina* gently took to the sea. The
edge of the water curled up, all white, tossing jumpropes
of spray toward us, as in some unfamiliar game.

The wind began to blow. Manuel took his seat in the
boat and with one oar veered it leftward, toward the
Descent.

"Let's get away from here," said my cousin.

"Let me go, you're hurting me . . ."

But he did not let me go. Manuel was no longer there,
not anyone, not even the *Leontina*. Only the two of us
and the wind, which suddenly flung a wave of sand up
against our faces—we felt it crunching between our

teeth. It was all like a dream, like a big lie in the style of Lauro the Chink. It was almost unbelievable.

The two of us approached the *Young Simón* at the same time, as if we needed some proof that everything was not false. Borja squatted and ran his finger over the warped worn wood, greyed by time. The black stain and the holes made by the two bullets were clearly visible. He squatted for a while without moving; finally he put a finger in one hole, then in the other. As I watched him, I remembered what they said about Saint Thomas, who put his fingers in the wounds of Jesus to convince himself of the truth. Everything seemed so unreal that afternoon. I stooped over and put my hand on his shoulder. He said:

"Well, I suppose he's going to return it."

"Should we wait?"

"Yes, what else can we do? Grandmother better not find out, no matter what. And we're not going to climb up there!"

I looked up toward the height, where the rocks darkened so much they seemed black and the pitas had a ferocious air, like cutlasses. Much further up, toward the sky, the trees got darker.

"But we can make it back home jumping from one rock to another."

"No," he persisted. "He has to bring the boat back. I told him to. He won't dare disobey . . ."

The gull flew over our heads and rushed at us stupidly. Borja began to clean the sand off his legs. We climbed inside the *Young Simón,* and stretched out. The sun was reddening in a clear sky; flies and a thousand insects were noisily buzzing. The sea sounded in a thick and monotonous murmur.

"The worst is going to be the stains," said my cousin.

"They'll rub out. Anyway, neither grandmother nor your mother ever come here, and they don't even remember the *Leontina.*"

Borja was silent a moment, and said:

"It isn't only . . . Well now, no one must know about this. Not the boys or anyone. No one should help those people. No one helps them. A few days ago, they harvested the crops by themselves . . . Everyone is afraid to help them because Malene and her people . . . well, they're marked, they're in a bad light."

He paused, always looking away at some remote point, and added:

"At times I've seen him digging in their orchard."

"I have too," I said. Without naming him, we both thought only about Manuel, and the image of him, suddenly very clear, stayed with me. Before this, I had never paid any attention to him. I never even asked the boys the question: "And the one from the house next door, who's he?"

"Who is he?" I asked now. "And why . . ."

"Because"—Borja made a vague gesture with his hand —"they're bad people. His father, the one they killed, was the administrator of Son Major . . . And they say the master married him off to his mistress, Malene, you know, Manuel's mother. The master gave them the house, the olive trees, the orchard . . . They owe everything to him."

"Jorge?" I asked maliciously, because I knew this was a weak spot in my cousin. If there was anyone my cousin admired from a distance it was Jorge of Son Major. He wanted to imitate him, to be like him some day. He wanted people some day to say things about him like those they said about our mysterious relative, who lived at the end of the village, at the corner of the cliff, secluded, never seeing anyone, with an old foreign man-servant named Sanamo. From what I heard from Antonia and Ton, Jorge of Son Major was an odd type, an adventurer who had squandered his fortune in an absurd way—according to grandmother—in strange and sinful voyages around the islands. But in the eyes of my cousin he was a fantastic being, and nothing less. Grandmother and Jorge had been estranged for many years.

"Well, that's the one," answered my cousin.

"What did José Taronjí do?"

"I've already told you that he was of bad birth, a bad man. He was Jorge's administrator, but he got himself talked about, and lately, I suppose, went without work. He was an ingrate, after all that Jorge did for them. He hated Jorge, he hated him with all his soul. And the Chink said he had the lists and that between them all they would divide up Son Major! Then, well, now you've seen it: they carried him off to some place and he wanted to get away . . . And they had to kill him."

Suddenly, those words took on a strange emphasis. He

must have realized it himself because he shut up quickly and his silence weighed on us. The sun still glared down, and in the silence, for a spell—in a way similar to what happens when one's eyes are closed and yet the bright outlines of objects are still visible and change color under the eyelids—I heard his voice saying: "They had to kill him, they had to kill him." The whole burnished crystal brilliance of the sky seemed to get inside our eyes, while the heavy heat fell on our bodies. I felt a queer emptiness in my stomach, something that was not only physical: perhaps because of having seen the dead man, the first dead man I had seen in my life. And I recalled the night in which I arrived on the island, the iron bed and its shadow on the wall behind me.

"I'm going to get a sunstroke . . ."

I sat down on the boat. Borja remained stretched out, silent and motionless. I could still see a shiny glare. I had it so far inside me, that everything—I myself, the dead boats, the sand, the prickly pears—all seemed sunken in the depths of an enormous and painful light. The sea sounded as if the waves were a fire which would flood me with thirst. A good deal of time must have gone by.

I jumped to the ground and went toward the golden shells. Then Borja called me:

"Come here, don't be stupid! If someone goes by up there, they can see you, and it's better no one knows . . ."

I came back. He had turned over, face downwards, and put his hand through the hatchway. Apparently, he wanted to act as if nothing had happened. At least, as if we had forgotten it.

He took out the cards. We sat down with our legs crossed, as usual. He lit the flashlight and hung it from the cable. It was still not night. I won twice, and the sky darkened. In any case, I still owed him money. My debts with him would never end! Borja took out the bottle, but we had no desire to drink. We took a swallow, even though we did not want it, and he put the bottle back. It was the horrible, sickeningly sweet liquor. We could no longer see. The flashlight, yellow, like an illuminated tongue, appeared to be surrounded by greedy insects, colliding into one another. The mosquitoes bit us; we slapped at them, and the noise of our slapping, as we hit our arms and legs, sounded in the night. Suddenly it occurred to me to ask:

"How long have they been like that?"

"Who?"

"Those . . . how long have they thought that way?"

"How do I know? They're full of spite. The Chink says . . . They're envious of us because we live decently. They're rotten with spite and envy. They'd hang all of us, if they could."

It was a theme that always worried me, because my father, apparently, was with them *on the other side.* Borja sometimes mortified me with allusions to my father and his ideas. But Borja seemed to have forgotten it for the moment. He continued:

"Just look and see if they're not a bad lot: Jorge helped them so much." (And I noticed how, when speaking of *them,* he insistently thought only of José Taronjí and his family.) "He kept Manuel in a convent, living and studying there. Everything paid, everything . . . Well, I don't know how they've got the nerve to come out of their house. And still, my father is risking his life because of people like that. My father, fighting at the front against those types . . . And I'm here, all alone."

He said these last words quickly, almost in a whisper. It was the first time I heard him use that phrase: *all alone*. It was strange. Of course, we could not see each other's faces, scarcely our hands, because of the flashlight. And that was the way it was, in twilight or darkness—just as when we jumped to the loggia at night, in pajamas, to go on with an interrupted card game or to talk and talk—when he dropped his arrogant and bullying air. It seemed to me that he was very much alone; I was alone, too, and perhaps, if it had not been for that solitude, we never would have been friends. I do not know what devil bit me at times—as when I was in Our Lady of the Angels—so that if something scratched me inside I would be pushed to wickedness. I felt like humiliating him:

"Don't complain, you have Lauro the Chink."

He did not answer and took out his cigarettes. In the darkness the tiny flame of the match glowed.

"Give me one," I asked, in spite of myself. On other occasions he would always haggle with me about them.

But he gave me one. It was a black and bitter tobacco, which he bought in the Café de Es Mariné.

"I want one of the others."

To my surprise, I saw that he searched carefully in the box and gave me one of the coveted *Murattis* that belonged to Aunt Emilia. We smoked in silence, until he said:

"Do you think it's wrong?"

"What?"

"Letting him take the boat."

I thought about it a moment:

"Grandmother wouldn't like it. Nor Lauro."

"Bah, Lauro!"

"He always says he hates them. He's always full of stories about their crimes and all that."

"That's what he says, but I don't believe it. Do you know what? He's like them. The same. The same as them. He's full of envy . . . I really hate them. I hate them with a vengeance."

I realized that his voice quivered slightly, as if he were afraid of something. He pressed his cigarette butt against the edge of the boat.

"Let's go. That fellow's not coming back . . . It's very late."

"Shouldn't we wait for him a little longer? Now it's worse to climb up there."

"We'll follow the rocks along the coast . . . He's a pig, that guy. Come on, hurry up. Lauro will be half-dead, hiding from grandmother."

He said this with a too-shrill little laugh. And he added, as if to himself:

"That Jew will pay for this!"

He put all the things away in the old raincoat, and hung the key to the box on the chain of his medal again.

(We had twin medals, gold, round, with the date of our birth stamped on them, a gift from grandmother. His medal represented the Virgin Mary and mine, Jesus. We never took them from around our necks, not even for sleeping. "It's the same as mine," he said, the first day we saw each other's. "With another saint . . ." We were looking at them, mine in his hand, his in mine. For an instant, it was as if we were brother and sister.)

Borja picked up a branch from the ground and slashed the reeds angrily. The noise of his slashing, the rumor of the sea, the waves breaking against the cliff filled the night. He helped me clamber along the rocks; but I scratched my legs and arms. With Borja it was useless to complain. I tried hinting:

"It'll be longer this way . . ."

"If you want, go on back," he answered, bad-humoredly.

But he knew that I had no alternative but to follow him. I asked myself why he dominated all of us: even the Guiems always accepted his terms. The sky was filled with large stars, and a violet light was rising. Slowly, from the sea, a greenish brilliance mounted. From time to time, Borja gave me his hand. At one point, where the rocks were wet, Borja slipped. I heard him swear.

"If grandmother knew you talked like that," I said. "She couldn't even imagine it!"

"Grandmother doesn't imagine anything," he answered mysteriously.

He stopped and turned toward me. He focused the

flashlight on my face and began to laugh in that almost feminine way which irritated me so much. He said:

"Well now, I'm thinking about one thing: What's going to become of you? At fourteen, smoking and drinking like a truck driver, and always going around with boys! Grandmother doesn't know that either, does she?"

I tried to smile as much like him as I could:

"That's how it is, just like that."

I searched for something to shock him, and suddenly, it occurred to me.

"My father is also risking his life because of *you*."

In spite of himself, this stopped him short. He lowered the light, which dazzled me, and I made out his dark silhouette, surrounded by an aureole.

"Oh, all right, then. So now you're with *them!*"

I didn't answer. He never had asked me about it. The truth was that I was surprised, too, by what I said. There was something that prevented me from acting and thinking for myself. To obey Borja, to disobey grandmother: that was my only preoccupation in those days. And then there were the perpetually confusing questions which no one could answer. Without knowing why, the memory of the forged-iron shadows and ants on the wall came back to me. There was something prison-like, something terribly sad in everything around me. And everything was summed up in the feeling I had on my first night on the island: someone was planning a bad time for me, on some vague date, and I could not fathom it at all. To my left the rocks rose, black, toward the slope of the mountains and woods. Below, the sea shimmered. I felt, as on so many other occasions, a strange fear. They could not leave me like this, in the middle of the world, so abandoned and ignorant. It just could not be.

"Evidently," I said.

(It was a word that I heard Lauro the Chink use a great deal when he spoke with grandmother.) Borja traced a circle of light. Then, he drew his hand across my face in an annoying gesture. I felt his hand grazing my cheek and forehead. I knew he did that to Guiem once in order to humiliate him, when they fought and he had pinned him up against the wall.

I insulted him with a word whose significance I did not understand. His hand stopped short.

"Your papa must have taught you these things, didn't he?"

I felt like lying. I felt like inventing stories, fiendish stories about my father (so unknown, so ignored; I did not even know if he fought at the front, if he collaborated with the enemies, or if he had fled to another country). I had to invent a father for myself, as a weapon, against something or someone. Yes, I knew it. And I understood, suddenly, that I had been inventing without knowing it for nights and nights, and days and days. I smiled knowingly:

"What would you know about it! You think you're very clever . . . Bah, if you only knew how sorry I am for you! You're very innocent. What I could tell you!"

I was getting used to the dark again and I saw Borja's

eyes gleam. He took me by the arm and pushed me along briskly.

At that instant, I did not hate him, nor did I feel the slightest rancor against him. But once started, it was very difficult to check my tongue. I said:

"You're really unhappy."

"Unhappy and all," he answered, "you just obey me. And poor, poor you, if you don't."

He put his face close to mine. I noticed that he stood on tiptoe, because if there was something that mortified him, it was my height. I was too tall for my age, I was taller than he and all the boys of both gangs. (I believe he never forgave me this.)

"What does Lauro the Chink do?" he said mockingly. "What does he do with me, my professor and preceptor?"

"You take advantage of ugly things, like that about poor Lauro . . . You have him in your clutches!"

"What do you know about it?"

I managed to laugh with an enigmatic air, as he often did, because I really didn't know anything. And I boasted:

"I'll go away from here soon. Sooner than all of you imagine."

In spite of himself, he was intrigued.

"When?"

"I don't think I'll tell you when. There are lots of things you don't know."

"Bah!"

He turned his back and began to walk again, feigning disinterest in my words. The yellow light of the flashlight slowly licked the holes and gaps of the rocks. Very carefully I followed the silhouette of his delicate ankles and feet, so as to put mine down in the same place.

When we arrived at the bottom of the Descent it was night. We let ourselves down to the pier in one jump, and Borja quickly lit it up with his flashlight. Tied in its usual spot was the *Leontina*.

"He's returned it . . . Look at it, Borja, there it is!"

"Why didn't he bring it back to Santa Catalina, as I ordered?"

And making a half-turn, he hastily climbed the little staircase.

There was something solemn about the Descent at night. The stones of the retaining walls whitened like rows of sinister heads in ambush. There was something human about the trunks of the olive trees; and the almonds, ready to be harvested, cast broad shadows. Beyond the trees, the glow of the tenant farmers' dwellings could be made out. At the end of the Descent the silhouette of grandmother's house made a denser shadow. The sky was tinted greenish and mauve.

The water slapped up against the sides of the *Leontina*. We had barely clambered a few yards when Borja shone his light on the first olive tree. Seated, yellowish in the glare of the light, was the Chink waiting patiently.

"Ah!" said my cousin. "You're here!"

Whenever he was taken unaware, there was something dark and concentrated in the Chink that was fearful.

"We'll tell your grandmother that we were taking a

walk . . . It was a beautiful afternoon to hold class in the open air. Do we all agree?"

Borja shrugged his shoulders. We climbed in silence, and I looked with a vague fear toward the right of the Descent, where the orchard and the white block of Manuel's house were surrounded by a low wall. Manuel Taronjí, Malene, and the little ones, María and Bartolomé. The dead man would be with them . . . I quivered and stopped among the trees. We had entered the area of the almonds. A penetrating odor rose from the earth, and further on, to the right, like an opaque star, glittered the light of an oil lamp or lantern. "Manuel's house," I repeated to myself.

"Let's go, quickly, if you please," insisted the Chink, in a smothered voice.

The windows of the tenant farmers' houses were illuminated, and surely grandmother would be spying from her boudoir with her opera glasses. I felt a dull grievance against her. She would be there, like a big-bellied and burnished god, like an enormous and gluttonous puppeteer moving the strings of her marionettes. From her boudoir, the tiny houses of the tenant farmers with their yellow lights, with their women cooking and their clamorous children, were like a miniature theater. She would be enveloping them in her hard, grey, dauntless look. Her eyes, like long tentacles, penetrated the houses, licked and swept the rooms, under the beds and tables. She had eyes which guessed, which raised the white roofs and lashed out at things: intimacy, sleep, fatigue.

We reached the level of the tenant farmers' houses. Across a door with a curtain half-drawn, light filtered through, and I said to myself: "All of them know about José Taronjí." There was something that floated in the heat, among the glistening mosquitoes, even in the clattering sound of a dish breaking inside the house with no scolding voice to follow it, in the jet of water falling against the earth. All the noises confirmed me in the same idea. "They know it, they all know about José Taronjí." I looked again toward the right. From that height, the tiny light of Malene's house could no longer be distinguished. In a flash, I remembered Malene vividly; but more than herself, it was her head of hair I recalled. (One day, by the wall of her house, while she drew water from the well, I contemplated her from behind, bent over. Her hair had fallen loose. It was a head of thick hair, of an intense, flaming red; a red that could burn, if it were touched. Stronger, more intense than that of her son Manuel. It was a beautiful head of straight hair, blinding under the sun.)

4

Something had happened. Grandmother was not seated in her rocking chair in the boudoir, next to the open window; and the rocking chair rocked softly and alone in the slight breeze.

They were all downstairs, in the big living room, next to the loggia. When we came in, grandmother looked at the three of us sharply: first at Lauro the Chink, then at Borja, and finally, at me.

"Where were you all so late? Why didn't you say you were going out?"

Before the Chink could answer, she reproached him, as was her habit, in an icy manner, without looking at his face, as if she were directing herself to someone else. She said that we should not get back at such late hours, nor leave the house without her permission. The Chink listened and nodded his head weakly. Next to the door, Antonia stood quietly, inexpressive, her eyes riveted, and her lips pressed together. She was wearing a black satin apron, with wide pleats, and one of those lace collars which she made herself. I imagined her heart pounding hard under her black dress every time grandmother scolded her son, but she was so calm and impassive that she seemed not to hear anything, nor notice Lauro's drooping head. My grandmother, seated in her armchair, speaking firmly, was chewing one of her innumerable lozenges. The neckline of her dress framed pleats and shirring gathered together with a velvet ribbon around her throat. Above the ribbon, pleats and shirring also rose toward her chin. She seemed to be shaped by the tight knot around her neck: her head above, her body below, like two purses, the head made of one material, the body of another. She still held in her hand one of her amber flasks, from which she had taken the lozenge. Seated at her side, as majestic as ever, was Monsignor Mayol, the priest of the Collegiate Church. Monsignor

Mayol played distractedly with a bluish crystal goblet, beautifully pearled, with opaque initials, like light through the rain. On clear nights he drank an orange liqueur, clear as water, and Pernod on cloudy nights, because he said drinks were directly related to the atmosphere or color of sky. (Amontillado for the glaring light of the sun, pristine or melancholy liqueurs for twilight.) When he said this, I tasted violent perfumes on my palate and felt a light dizziness. Above grandmother and Monsignor Mayol, looking out of his grandiose frame, was grandfather in his uniform of something very important —I never knew what exactly, even though it was repeated to me many times, I suppose—and his blue or red sash (I don't remember which). On the little table, in its silver frame, was the photograph of Uncle Álvaro. He looked like Borja, in spite of his hard ugliness. (The two of them, grandfather and Uncle Álvaro, were almost physically in the room. Their eyes could not be ignored, nor their jaws, whenever we gathered in that room: grandfather's wide and spongy, the other's sharp and cruel. Borja's father's long and lean face, capped by his big Carlist beret, with a scar on the right-hand corner of his mouth, and all the rest of the portraits of ex-princes, aspirants to kingship or ex-infantes, dedicated in writing to Uncle Álvaro, always participated at our gatherings.) Aunt Emilia, seated a little apart, near the loggia, lifted the curtain with one hand. Outside, it was dark. Only the tiny lights of fireflies glowed in the garden. Aunt Emilia was always like that: as if waiting for something;

as if lying in ambush; as if she might have been saturated in some mysterious and unfamiliar substance. "Like a big rum-soaked pastry," I thought once, "which seems vacuous and innocent, but still is soaked in liquor." Aunt Emilia spoke very little. Borja would sometimes say: "Mamma is sad, she's worried about Papa." She and her husband were for me, in those days, like a mystery I could not penetrate. Except for playing the piano badly, and almost always the same pieces, I never saw her do anything. She did not even read the newspapers and magazines which she piled around herself in great heaps; she glanced at them, distractedly, and it was obvious that even if her eyes lingered a long time on a photograph her thoughts were far away. She had tiny blue eyes, with a pinkish cornea, and she was forever spying through the windows or looking toward the patio through the hollow of the staircase. At times, I thought: "She's not sad." Sometimes she went to the city in the morning and came back at night. She usually brought me some gift, and I recall that on one of these trips she bought me some very pretty silk pajamas; thanks to those pajamas I was able to banish the horrible school nightgowns. She treated grandmother in the same suave manner as Borja did. It was difficult to think of her loving Uncle Álvaro. He seemed to be there in his photograph, with his decorations, but we knew that he was at the front, "killing enemies and having soldiers shot if they don't obey." (Borja would say: "My father is a colonel and can have anyone he wants to shot.") But he was as good as dead, really. As dead as grandfather himself. We had scarcely heard from him in two months: only some vague news and telegrams.

Monsignor Mayol opened the newspaper and pointed out the headlines. Another city had just been conquered. Lauro the Chink blushed:

"It has fallen . . . It has fallen . . ." he said.

Everyone began to talk at the same time. Grandmother smiled, baring her eyeteeth, something that rarely happened, because she usually smiled—the few times she ever did—with her mouth closed. Tightening her lip over her sharp teeth, she had the same look as Borja had in his other life, the one outside of the house. "Perhaps grandmother is concealing another life also, far from us." But I could not imagine her consorting vulgarly with the people in the village.

From outside came something like a murmur, low and warm, and it bloused out the curtain. On the little table, the newspapers acquired an unexpected life; they flapped their strange wings and squabbled under the hand of the priest, which fell flat and heavily on them.

"Wind," said grandmother. "The wind has come up again! I was afraid it would."

Grandmother knew the sky, and almost always could read its signs. The curtain flew in Aunt Emilia's face, and the two fought torpidly. The curtain seemed something alive, and they wrangled in a singular battle. Borja ran to her side, and freed her from the nuisance. She was very pallid and her lips trembled. I looked at the garden. There below, two wrinkled papers blew, chasing each other like animals. Grandmother continued speaking, behind me:

"Tomorrow, at eleven, Monsignor Mayol will celebrate a *Te Deum*. Everyone in this house will attend Santa María to give thanks to God for this victory of our troops . . ."

The lamp began to waver, and grandmother said:

"Close the balcony doors."

Lauro the Chink went over to the balcony. His yellow profile stood up toward the sky beyond the arches of the loggia. Then, he extended his arms in a cross toward the leaves of the door. Aunt Emilia went to sit down next to the vicar.

Borja offered me a chair and remained at my side, on foot, like a little soldier. His hair was still damp, just combed. Quiet, erect, and delicate, he was watching grandmother with his enormous pale green eyes. The bamboo cane slid and fell to the floor. Borja rushed to pick it up. The light shone on the top of the cane and its reflection ran across the wall, swiftly, like a golden insect.

Antonia opened the dining room door all the way. Dinner was served. The doctor, who was a widower, the priest, the vicar and Juan Antonio were eating with us. Juan Antonio was a bit older than we, but no one could have guessed it by his height. He was very thin and greenish-skinned; his eyes were set very close together. A repulsive, blackish down grew above his lip, and his hands, stubby and fat, were always moist. He confessed himself three or four times a week, and then meditated for a long time before the altar, with his head between his hands. (One day I saw him crying in church. Borja told me: "When he gets like that it's because he's sinned a lot. That guy's a big sinner." And then he clarified: "He sins a lot against the sixth commandment, you know? He's very dishonest and surely he'll be condemned. He goes and confesses, but he knows very well he'll sin again, because he can't help himself. The devil has him neatly cornered." "How do you know all that?" I asked. "Sometimes we talk . . . But I . . ." he elucidated, "I'm not involved in all this." He began to laugh maliciously, and I also laughed, trying to half-close my eyes as he did.) And there was Juan Antonio, serious and taciturn, as always spied on by his Friendly Enemy, the Devil. He was a glutton and ate in a sloppy way. He slobbered his food along the edge of his lips, and just looking at him was nauseating, but it was impossible to keep one's eyes off him. And he was the best friend and comrade of Borja. Because Borja said he was very intelligent, more so than Carlos and León, the sons of the administrator.

Because of the wind, they closed the windows and it got very hot. Monsignor Mayol's forehead was encircled with sparkling drops, like a crown. The priest was tall and very handsome. He must have been about fifty years old, and his hair was white, and his large eyes were brown. The Chink blushed every time the priest said a word to him. Monsignor Mayol brought the napkin to his lips very delicately, and patted them lightly.

Monsignor Mayol possessed a great sense of dignity, and to me he seemed the most elegant and good-looking man I had ever seen. "He is very handsome," said grandmother. "He officiates with the dignity and majesty of a prince. There is nothing comparable to the Catholic Liturgy!" And upon saying it, she seemed to predict a future of enormous possibilities for him: at least a cardinalship. Monsignor Mayol dressed in habits of coarse materials, which fell in ample pleats and swished in a special way when he walked. He was not a native of the island, and he walked with a certain slowness and abandon. Everyone said he was a very cultured man. When he came to eat—which happened frequently—he would pace the loggia afterwards for a long while, reading his breviary, with Borja at his side, whether he wanted it or not. He almost never directed a word to me, but often I felt the disapproving glance of his golden, cold and glittering eyes, like two coins. On the rare occasions on which he said something to me, he did it through grandmother or Borja. I felt very respectful in his presence, almost fearful; I believe I never saw him smile. Grandmother said that he was a great lover of music, and Aunt Emilia would talk with him, at times, of rare and antique scores and other things like that, which we could not understand. I almost took to sympathizing with Monsignor Mayol on the occasions when Borja's mother decided to cudgel the piano in his presence. Then, the small light of martyrdom could be detected in his eyes. Monsignor Mayol had a very sonorous voice, and his strong point, according to the Chink, was Gregorian chant: "To hear him is to draw near the doors of Glory."

Later that night the wind stopped, and when I looked out to the Descent, as I went to bed, a strong odor was rising from the earth. Down below, the sea gleamed. Suddenly a milky light spread out from behind the clouds, and I saw a curtain of rain descending upon us.

It rained all night, until dawn.

5

When I awoke—though I had not yet opened my eyes —I realized I was not alone. I felt a grazing, a rustle, as of wings. I slowly lifted my eyelids; my head was turned toward the wall, which was flooded with a yellow radiance. The sun entered in bands through those shutters which perturbed me because they could not be closed. (On the first morning I awoke in that room, when the pearled light of dawn seeped between the slats, I went to close them, and could not; I felt terribly frustrated and, since then, it had been very difficult for me to accustom myself to the dawn.)

Antonia was next to the window, with the parakeet Gondoliero, feeding him birdseed from her hand. Slowly I turned to look at her. She also looked at me, silently, and I sat up. I saw myself in the mirror of the wardrobe, divided by the whiteness of the sheets, with my hair loose and the sun bringing out its red cast.

"Let's go, child, it's late . . ."

I threw myself back. She added:

"I was looking at the way you slept, just before, and you reminded me of your mother."

It bothered me to have someone see me sleeping; I was so wrapped up in my dreams I thought they might be discovered, and I was so completely defenseless. It irritated me to hear her say:

"You don't ordinarily look like your mother, but when you sleep you do. When you sleep, Matia, I think it's she."

Gondoliero began to chatter in a sharp little voice, and Antonia slid her finger with immense delicacy over his striped head.

"You're thin, child; I'm afraid you might be sick."

"I'm not!"

"But I heard you calling out in your dreams," she continued, tiresomely, in her low and humble voice. "You were practically screaming . . ."

"Well, and what about it? I've always yelled at night. Mauricia knew it, and thought nothing of it."

Gondoliero flew from her hand, gave two turns in a low, clumsy flight, and perched on the canopy of the bed. He looked like an animated, anguished flower. I raised an arm to shoo him from there; my arm glistened in a ray of sunlight which crossed it. In the room, which had been my mother's, all the furniture was a very shiny, reddish mahogany, though it glowed like cherry wood.

"Do you know?" she went on. "Your mother also used to scream at night."

"My mother, always the same story. No one knows anything about my mother! Why is everyone forever telling me about her?" I jumped to the floor and stretched my feet in the sun, which fell in patches on the inlaid floor. It was warm.

I heard the door smoothly opened, and Aunt Emilia came in.

"Hurry up, Matia," she said.

She went up to the mirror, and Antonia began to gather up my scattered clothes from the floor. But I knew that she was listening attentively: it could almost be seen in her waxy snail-like ear. Aunt Emilia stared at herself in the mirror, running her hands across her cheeks, as if she were avidly searching out her first wrinkles. At that time she seemed to me a mature woman, but she must have been, at most, thirty-five. Her hair was blond, straight, and very brilliant. She had wide hips, like her jaws. She was not pretty but very soft, and was usually absent-minded and self-absorbed, as if she were always asking herself something that kept her in perpetual wonder.

The saint languished in his niche, between tuberoses and wax lilies; his eyes were an imploring crystal. The candles, half melted, twisted in the small candelabras, and a spider, brown and wary, crawled along the upper wall.

"Hurry up," she repeated distractedly. "Grandmother would bawl you out if she knew you were still in bed."

She left the room. She always did things like that: she

would enter, leave, speak without looking at your face, with the air of a sleepwalker. "She's like a phantom."

Antonia went into the adjoining room, which was a bathroom. I never saw a bathroom the likes of the one in grandmother's house: a big, shabby room with odd furniture of dark wood and marble. The enormous sink and the big, inclined mirror over it, where I was reflected in a sloping posture, as in a fantastic dream, looking at myself up and down, seemed more like a clothes closet. The room was lined with shelves of greenish crystal, covered with empty bottles and flasks. A dismal noise grumbled in the defective water pipes, warm in summer, icy in winter. The reddish marble of the sink, striped with bleeding veins, and the black of the wood with carved, interlaced dragons overwhelmed me. The first days of my stay I spent a long time in that odd lavatory—as Antonia always called it—putting my finger between the cracks in the horribly combined wood and marble, in which there was perpetual dust. The bathtub was old and chipped, with glazed, yellowish-white lions' feet, and it had big black marks, like the stigmas of an evil race. Rust and moisture stains covered the walls, forming queer continents, tears of age and abandon. The really hot water Antonia had to bring from the kitchen in porcelain pitchers. I heard her bustling around and imagined her, as always, between clouds of steam which blurred the mirror and lent it a still more unreal and enigmatic air. "Alice through the Looking Glass," I thought, on more than one occasion, looking at myself in it, nude and disconsolate, longing to penetrate its surface, which seemed gelatinous. What a sad image it was —my own—with those frightened eyes! It was the image, perhaps the very picture, of solitude.

Antonia had turned red, while Gondoliero, perched on her right shoulder, was desperately blue.

I sat down on the edge of the bed and swung my legs. The high bed, as if hung from the ceiling, made me dizzy. When I dozed I imagined it was a boat floating in a sea of clouds, on its way to some place I did not want to reach. I was still wearing the rough white nightgown from the School of Our Lady of the Angels, with its numbers embroidered in red on the right shoulder: 354, 3rd, A. I felt like the number of an apartment. The shadows of Antonia and Gondoliero appeared on the wall.

"Where did you and Borja go?" asked Antonia, looking at my sunburned legs, covered with scratches, and the adhesive tape on my right knee.

"Over there," I answered yawning.

She came closer, buried her hands in my hair and began to run it through her fingers, as if it were a jet of water.

"Not one curl, not one wave . . ." she continued.

Gondoliero perched on the bedspread and then romped on the canopy. Antonia put her hands on my shoulders:

"How thin you are! You're sick, poor child. They ought to take care of you. Yes, yes, God knows they ought to take care of you."

Who, I thought, were the mysterious beings that ought

to take care of me? Surely, she could not be referring to grandmother.

"I'm not sick! What a nag you are!"

At ten-thirty we left for Santa María. The sun blazed fiercely and the garden was hardly damp. Only a puddle, in which a few birds pecked, gave evidence of the night's storm. Grandmother indicated the bushes and flowers with her cane, commenting on them to Aunt Emilia. They both wore mantillas of blonde lace, and grand-mother, her double strand of pearls. Aunt Emilia wore a suit of shiny black silk, which accentuated the wide-ness of her hips. Grandmother, gazing at Borja, said:

"It's a shame boys grow up. At this age they can't be dressed like men or like boys. There's nothing to com-pare with sailor suits! Isn't that so, Emilia? Do you re-member what a dream Borja was in his white sailor suit? It seems only yesterday!"

I smiled out of the corner of my eye at Borja, and he dedicated one of his sweetest looks to grandmother, while he gritted between his teeth: "You, inside your corset, trapped like a whale."

The garden was very neglected, and grandmother was lamenting the fact.

"But," she said, "these are bad days to be thinking about things like these. We're living in days of austerity and restrictions."

The iron gate was open and Ton, with his straw hat in his hand, was watching us. One of his eyes was clouded over and he was missing two teeth. Looking at

him, I recalled: *She'll defend me, she'll defend me.*
Grandmother passed solemnly in front of him, making
the ground crunch. She had the most improbably small
feet, but she left imprints in the earth, still softened by
the rain. The sun made the leaves of the fig tree glimmer.
I approached it, slowly, my eyes riveted on the very top.
(Yes, there was the cock, quiet and white.) The fig tree
was still wet, with miniature clusters of drops shining on
the back side of the most concealed leaves. The yellow
shadow of the house weighed on me. At that moment the
golden shadow lit up the fig tree and made it shine
afresh. And there was the mysterious runaway cock of
Son Major, white and flashing. His angry eyes, raised
over the branches, glared at us defiantly. Grandmother
called:

"Matia! Matia!"

I turned around slowly. An odd sensation of bewilderment and fear encompassed me. Grandmother was
turned toward me, like a black, round mass, like a stone
about to be rolled.

"Matia! Matia!"

She continued calling, or at least it seemed so to me: I
could not tell. The sun, very close to me, was agitating
a strange fire in the tree, in the leaves, in the round
pupils of the cock. I lifted my eyes and the sky was not
red, as it had seemed, but rather was like a tin roof moist
from the rain.

"Matia!"

Grandmother looked at me out of her smoke-rimmed
eyes, under the white wave of hair which shone in the

sun. (Antonia would say: "What a beautiful head of hair the mistress has.") Antonia (with her veil almost covering her eyes and her freckle, which was like a spider on top of her lip) said:

"She's not well. Even last night she looked pale to me. This girl is not well."

The Chink came up close to me. A tiny sun was reflected in the green crystals of his glasses.

"Miss Matia, I beg you to hurry. Your grandmother is waiting for you. The *Te Deum* is scheduled for eleven."

Then I turned around to see them, grouped in front of the iron gate, waiting for me. I looked to the left, toward the beginning of the village and the first houses of the plaza. The cupola of green mosaics glittered in the sun, as if it were gilded. It was a flaming green, cruel at morning time: like a scream.

"That cock from Son Major always comes here," I said. And I began to walk toward them.

"It certainly does," the Chink agreed. "It always comes here to that very tree."

"It's very mysterious," grandmother said.

We crossed through the iron gate, and Ton, with his white eye, stared at me intently, cruelly.

"That girl," Aunt Emilia was saying to grandmother, "is ill, poor thing. We have to watch her . . ."

"Ah, yes." Grandmother suddenly raised her two hands and held her mantilla for one moment on top of her white wave. "These poor children haven't had the luck to live in a decent period . . . We're ruined, and there's a war! Good God, Almighty God, what grief!"

The bell of Santa María began to toll, like an avalanche of screams over the village, in a startling manner: like shreds of words, like a thousand laments scattered in the air or discordant complaints. (They awoke the silence, which was only trodden by the black boots of the Taronjís.)

We went through the artisans' quarter, behind the plaza. It was quiet, and Borja slid on the polished stones.

"Careful, my angel," said grandmother.

The Chink took my cousin by the elbow.

It was not Sunday but there was something about the day that made it seem so. The blacksmith's forge was silent. The shoemaker's cubicle and the Taronjís' store had the wood shutters drawn down over the window and showcase. In front of us, a woman in black, throwing her veil over her head, ran, as if she wanted to catch the last peals of the bell. The street opened upon the small plaza of the church with its central fountain from which the pigs drank and to which the children clambered to splash the women, and where my grandmother's pigeons perched, crossing through the village, toward Son Major, like blue flashes of lightning. Behind the fountain rose Santa María, big and golden. The doors of the church were open, and the last of the faithful ascended the stone steps. Suddenly, the bell stopped and there was a burst of silence. Between Aunt Emilia and the Chink, grandmother was helped up the steps. They took her, each one by an arm, as if they were raising a big earthen jar by its handles, with infinite care, so as not to spill the oil. (And that was grandmother: a rich substance that everyone esteemed, even if the jar was old and ordinary.)

At the church door several men took off their hats and some of the women bowed their heads. Borja and I, hand in hand, followed them. The seam of Aunt Emilia's right stocking was twisted.

Over the arch of the big gilded door, which was open, there were escutcheons of stone and the heads of the four evangelists. On top of the cupola of green mosaics, extracting an evil flame from them, was the sun, red and fierce in the middle of the pallid sky. And I said to myself: "The sky is almost never blue." A cruel sensation of violence, an irritated fire blazed there above: everything was steeped and saturated in that black light. Clusters of iron glistened in the doorjambs. Inside, the greenish-black humidity, like that of a well, stuck to one's body. In the enormous palate of Santa María there was something like a solemn fluttering of wings. And I told myself that perhaps in the darkness of the corners bats nested, that there were rats fleeing and chasing one another among the gold of the altarpieces. Grandmother's house was also somber and dirty. (Antonia complained that it was too big for only two women, and only the rooms that were lived in were cleaned.) There were cobwebs and dust on the porcelain, the silver, and the dishes that the king had given to great-grandfather when he married. And in the glass case, around the tiny shining statues of jade, and above, in the enormous and

mysterious bathroom (with its tilted, cloudy mirror like
the door to a complicated world, and its noise of pipes
which always burst in winter), and below, in the orchard,
with the ants; and in the whole house with its leaks and
drafts, there, in the corners of the nave, was the same
moist wind. And in grandmother's house was the same
mixture of odors: wood, mold, salt. And the flowers.
(Some red gladioli bloomed beyond the yellow wall
of the house covered with honeysuckle, by the tiny stone
stairway, where I usually sat when Borja did not want
to take me along.) Inside Santa María, the fascinating
stained-glass windows exploded their color among the
blackness and mold, high and glittering in the darkness,
and avidly licked by the sun. Especially the one depicting
the thin saint whose hands were joined and nailed.
A ray of luminous red fell on the floor like a bloodstain.
And a flash of sunlight, just like a gold butterfly, flew
from one side of the vault to the other. Monsignor Mayol
sang:

"De-um Lau-da-mus: te Dominum confite-mur . . ."

Grandmother pushed me along, discreetly but without
any gentleness. Her fingers dug into my right shoulder.
Then she took the book from my hands. It was a thick
missal given to me when I entered Our Lady of the
Angels, with gilt-edged pages that I used to rub with
the tips of my fingers because they gave off a fine
dust, like the kind from butterfly wings, which I rubbed
against my eyelids and teeth (but I never managed to get
it to stick to my teeth). She opened the missal at the
green ribbon, and said: "Read." The sun shone outside

like a silent red thunderclap, much stronger than any explosion. I raised my eyes to the stained-glass windows, unable to read. There was the little saint that looked like Borja, with curls like bunches of grapes, and a powerful Saint George, massive and radiating gold, above a slaughtered dragon. The Chink and Borja were reading devotedly in their missals.

"... *Ti-bi che-ru-bim et se-ra-phim in-ces-sa-bi-li vo-ce procla-mant: San-ctus San-ctus Sanctus ...*"

The Chink once said that the priest's cope was three hundred years old. It was white, with borders and fringes of gold which flashed in the darkness (like the open, majestic wings of the Son Major cock, which were still soaked from the storm, atop the velvety leaves).

My right leg was asleep and I rubbed it with my left ankle. Grandmother passed the missal to me and looked at me sternly. I bent my head over the book and closed my eyes. I was hungry. In all the rush I had not had time for breakfast. I told myself that when I grew up I would do the same as Aunt Emilia, who smoked languidly in bed until noon, looking at the photographs and headlines in the newspapers. All the voices were suddenly raised. The sun reverberated through the colored glass, as if it wanted to pierce the window. Above the black palate of the nave was the sun, and we, I thought, like Jonah, were inside the whale, with its enormous ribs. I imagined the burning green of the cupola, like a big gold-and-rainbow jigsaw puzzle.

"... *Te marty-rum candi-da-tus laudat ex-er-ci-tus ...*"

"The war," I said to myself, "what kind of thing is it, really?" Everything was so quiet. And that boy asking us for the boat. And the Taronjís. They said they were cousins: the boy was called Manuel Taronjí. And Malene, with her beautiful red hair, soft and long, in the sun. Always the sun, there above. And Uncle Álvaro. And my father? And my mother? "She also screamed at night." Well, so what? They never came to see me. ("Your parents were divorced, weren't they?" Juan Antonio asked me, while both of us were seated on the stone stairway, below the honeysuckle. "It's not true." But he laughed maliciously, and I did not understand why. He put his hand on my knee and began to caress it. My skirt went up a bit, only a bit: I saw my sunburned knee, round and soft—never, until that moment, had it occurred to me that it could be so pretty—and suddenly, I could not stand his sweaty hand. He said: "Your mother . . ." I was obsessed by his hand, which repelled me as if it were a toad. And he had such repulsively red lips! I gave him a brutal shove and he fell against the wall. The flowers beside us gave off a strong perfume. From below a jet of green light reached us, as if the sea itself were there, just around the corner from grandmother's house. But it was not true.) My mother was an unknown woman, only an unknown woman. And I, after her death, so long ago, in the country house which grandmother said was falling to pieces, was then living with my father's old nanny. Packages of toys would arrive: the Children's Theater and that rag clown as tall as myself; and that story: *"'Why have we no immortal souls?' asked the Little Mermaid sadly."* She did not have one, she did not have one, and she turned into foam. *"Every step she took was, as the witch had warned her beforehand, as if she were treading on sharp knives and spikes . . ."*

". . . quos pre-ti-o-so sanguine rede-mis-ti . . ."

The Little Mermaid wanted to be loved, but no one ever loved her. Poor mermaid! Was it necessary then for her to be like a human? But she was not a woman. I lifted my eyes and searched for some prayer. "My friends . . ." I began to say; and I cut myself off. "What friends, God of Armies, what friends are those?"

(Perhaps I only wanted someone to love me for once. I cannot remember very well.)

6

At the mayor's house there were "refreshments." At least they were called that.

We went there after church. The two Taronjí brothers were there, even if the younger one—according to the Chink—*did not properly have any official duty.* Monsignor Mayol, the mayor, his wife, some other village big shots, and the vicar were all in attendance.

Monsignor Mayol and grandmother reigned; they were disdainful and silent. We arrived at the mayor's house, courted by all of them, surrounded by their voices and reverences. Then, in the patio, we gathered around a table covered with sparkling glassware. The Chink stood apart, glass in hand, harassed by a couple of flies.

The wine was horrible; it was sweet and left our lips sticky. Borja and I looked at each other out of the corner of our eyes and he made a face, puckering his lips and pulling them down. The mayor's wife had planted a grapevine in the patio and grandmother pointed it out.

"Who thought of that?" she asked, vaguely envious.

And her finger indicated the pergola where the miniature, pale green bunches of grapes were almost indistinguishable from the leaves. Someone looked up and began to talk about when they would ripen. Borja and I sat down on a bench, next to the whitewashed stone wall. Grandmother spoke with the mayor, and continued talking even when the Taronjís twice tried to direct a word to her. But she pretended not to see them.

The Chink continued to stand apart, quietly. At last, one of the flies fell in his glass. The mayor's wife hovered around the table like a buzzing horsefly. The sun fell into the patio as into a well. The table was covered with a white linen tablecloth; its creases were very marked, as if it had been stored away for years without ever having been spread out. The blue crystal goblets also seemed filled to bursting with the raging sun, mixed with the brilliance of the wine, red like mahogany. Under the bench, at our feet, a row of ants opened a way for themselves. Borja killed them slowly, one by one. The mayor's wife passed around a tray of pastry. They spoke of the war, of the victory. Over the balcony the flag fell flaccidly, without any wind.

Voices sounded behind the wall, but the people in the patio heard nothing. Borja stood up on the bench, and I imitated him. The top of the wall was bristling with small pieces of broken bottle glass, sharp as teeth, ready to rip into the flesh. ("The same as the ones at Son Major," said the elder Taronjí, looking at grandmother and drawing himself up in his malodorous military jacket.)

We saw them between the sharp pieces of glass, which came exactly up to the level of my eyes. The three of them went down the road: Malene, her son Manuel, and the little boy. They walked in silence, their shoes covered with clay, as if they might have come from some gloomy place, from scratching under the crust of the earth, where the heavy rain of the storm still had not dried. They disappeared behind the evergreen oaks and once again appeared, closer still. They wore their usual clothes, not mourning. Side by side they came into the street. As if waiting for them, Guiem's mother, the wife of the black-smith, and two other women, whose voices began to rise shrilly, came out into the street. But they—Malene, Manuel and the boy—said nothing, and when they had passed silence was reborn, in a strange, almost magical way. I could no longer see anything through the row of sharp broken glass. Just then they crossed to the other side of the wall, and we heard only their footsteps on the stones of the street. Hardly were they out of sight when the irate voices of the blacksmith's wife and the other women were raised: "They ought to be ashamed—ex-hibiting themselves like that," they said. "Of course, they couldn't have given him a Christian burial . . ." "They wouldn't dare!"

"Their shoes are covered with clay," my cousin said in a dull voice, "but they're not coming from the cemetery . . . Where could they have buried him?"

The sun hurt my eyes, amid the green, opal, diamond-like splendor of the broken glass. I ran the tip of my finger gingerly across the knife-sharp edges. My eyes were aching from so much light.

The Chink approached us from behind:

"Get down, please . . . please . . ."

Borja landed on the ground in one jump. The sun turned green and ruby-red among that fierce set of teeth.

"Will the grapes do as well here . . . as in Son Major?" asked the mayor's wife in a cottony voice.

With two fingers, the Chink took the drowned fly out. He threw it in the air, and it stuck against the wall, oozing one golden drop.

THE *SCHOOL*
OF THE *SUN*

STORMS did not frighten me. I liked the thunder, sweeping across the village from the mountain to the sea, rolling down the Descent. But I was afraid of the wind, and before it came up, it reminded me of a slithering animal. I awoke in the darkness. The mirror shone and was like a breath traversing the room. At times, flowers blooming unexpectedly in small gardens and orchards behind the village houses frightened me in the same way: it was as if they heralded some mystery under the island, some kingdom, perhaps, beautiful and evil.

(One day I asked to go to the river's edge, and the Chink said: "There is not a single river on the island." Not one river, not one single river. If there was something lovely in my past life it was the green afternoons of the river, at siesta time, or twilight, or during the golden morning: the reeds, the canebrake, the smooth rocks along the shore, like tiny stone beaches.)

Behind Guiem's father's forge, behind the windows of

that small, blue-painted door which closed clumsily, was the orchard-garden Guiem's mother cultivated zealously. Guiem's mother was a fat woman who felt very flattered that Borja and I—even I—went to her house.

On the island I learned about the sun, which made the flowers in Guiem's garden shimmer, which filled the mist, and transmogrified it into a moist fire gradually evaporating over the chalices of the flowers. The island flowers were something extraordinary. I had never seen such big flowers or such vivid colors (those of my region were tiny wild flowers of a purple, white or terrified yellow color which grew among the high grasses, trees, and white dew). These flowers, on the other hand, as if sprung from the stones, dominated everything: the air, the light, the atmosphere. It seemed so unusual to me that they should grow there, from the earth, everywhere: in the path, in the Descent, next to the well of our house, with its dragon covered with moss and its wrought iron, red with rust. At times, when Borja decided to make peace for a few days, we went to the Guiem forge, to his orchard-garden.

Two days after the affair at Santa Catalina with Manuel, Borja took us up the street:

"We're going to the forge. I want to talk to Guiem."

"Is there going to be a truce?"

"Yes."

The Chink pretended to follow us, and it was painful to hear his hurried steps and panting behind us. "He has a tendency to bronchitis," Antonia had said.

Guiem helped his father. At the entrance to the forge,

even before, at the corner, the hammer blows could already be heard.

Borja walked ahead and went in. The Chink put a hand on my shoulder:

"Miss Matia, be good," he said. "I beg you both to be good."

I looked at him out of the corner of my eye, because I was embarrassed when he said things like that. And he added:

"You two don't understand. Afterwards, I have to explain to your grandmother. She doesn't like you to keep company with these types. Do you realize that?"

"Yes, I realize it," I said wearily.

And he added, with a strange fury:

"You're both pitiless, cruel . . . you don't understand anything. It's not for me, it's for her . . . do you understand? It's my mother: I don't want her to suffer for me . . . She's so alone! She taught that bird, Gondoliero, to go back and forth with her, when I went away to the Seminary, so as not to be so lonesome. Now that she has me here she can't stand your grandmother speaking to me rudely. You ought to understand that, but you don't want to. You don't want to! You're hard-hearted, God knows."

"You're talking idiocies! I don't understand anything about that bird or all the rest of it, and do me the favor of keeping your hand off me."

I, too, spoke with a kind of fury, a fury that surprised me. Or perhaps it was fear. Or was it an unlikely sensation, like sadness? How could I know? But I felt my heart squeezed down as at Our Lady of the Angels, with Gorogó under my pillow.

The blacksmith was there with his big, scarred leather apron. The Chink smiled:

"Can we go to the garden? The children want . . ."

"I don't expect anything has happened . . ."

"Nothing, nothing at all, goodness! The children . . ."

He signaled us with his hand and I saw his mother's silver ring on his little finger.

"He, his mother, his ring," I said to myself confusedly. "Them, always them. And me, nothing, no one, never." (True, I had a ring in the carved chest and grandmother told me that there were more in the bank. But I did not want them, I did not want them. When I grew up I would give them all away.)

"What a sight you were with that tunic, Chink," I said suddenly. "And why did you leave the Seminary? The priests didn't want you there, did they? You don't believe in God, Borja knows it very well."

There, again, were the enormous flowers, like a poison, the deeper we penetrated the little garden. (And why, why did I laugh and why was I so sad, saying that to the Chink? Why all the bitterness which I could even taste on my tongue?)

"All right, Matia, keep quiet. We're going to study a bit," my cousin said.

He sat down on the ground and opened the book on his knees.

"Go on, Chink, tell us about God," I insisted.

(I could not keep quiet because there was something

there, in the sun, the flowers and all the leaves, that made my tongue wag acidly.)

The Chink also opened his book. Then he took out the inevitable handkerchief in order to wipe his forehead. There was no more than the barest breeze. Upon seeing the embroidered initials on that handkerchief, a dark envy invaded me. Who embroidered it, if not his mother, the pale Antonia of the pursed lips? I tore a leaf between my fingernails. Idiotically, I wanted to say: "Well, even if I saw little of my mother, my father sent me toys and books and a clown, on the Day of the Three Wise Men . . ." But who was I going to talk to about the Three Wise Men—to Borja, to Guiem, to the Chink? I was terribly confused.

The little door of glass and wood, painted blue, opened into the room where Guiem's mother had the brazier table with its long-skirted cover sewn with dull flowers, and the radio with a cretonne slip cover, and the calendar, and the sewing machine. Sometimes Mauricia would say to me: *"Don't be afraid."* When? When did she tell me that? Was it true that she once told me that? I was a little girl, and suddenly . . .

"You don't deserve to know. Why tell you about Him?" the Chink said.

Borja raised his head and his eyes glittered:

"Ah, very well, Chink, do you want to go back to the Naranjal?"

The Chink tightened his lips. His shirt was dirty. Antonia had no time to wash it, probably because she was washing and ironing our clothes. ("How good!") It was like being inside a glass. The sky and atmosphere all seemed as if they were inside a bell glass. Two butterflies chased one another. My cousin said:

"And God, what does He say about Manuel Taronjí's father?"

"He certainly must think that he was a bad man. It's not good to let oneself be dominated by envy and hatred; all men ought to be satisfied with what God has provided for them."

"And what has He provided for you?"

Borja crushed an insect against a page of the book and dragged it with the tip of his finger, leaving a stain of brown blood.

He insisted:

"Chink, what has He provided for you?"

At that moment Guiem's mother came out: the glass in the door shook. She crossed her arms and smiled as she looked at us.

"My Lord, why do these children, with a garden as pretty as theirs, come to poor peoples' gardens? What does my garden have that theirs hasn't got?"

As she went on speaking, I thought about the rivers again. "Yes, of course there are rivers, rivers under the earth, as far as the sea." I closed my eyes and a red glow filtered between my eyelids. I heard Borja say:

"Can Guiem come? We're waiting for him to finish work."

I opened my eyes to see how she gloated:

"But, my Guiem . . . what is it that you always have to tell each other?"

Guiem stuck his hairy, rough head out of the door.
He said:

"I'm working. Wait for me there, Borja."

Borja slammed the book shut to trap a green butterfly
between the pages.

"We want to go to the Port. Will you come, Guiem?"

"The Port!" his mother said, raising her heavy arms
in the air. "And what business has Guiem got at the
Port?"

The Chink put his handkerchief back in his cuff. We
got up to leave. The air was red and black in the forge.
Half the blacksmith's body was dyed in darkness and the
other half in the bright red of the fire. From the wall,
from the blackened bricks, iron tools hung like instru-
ments of torture.

It was Saturday and behind Santa María the market
booths were being set up. The village vendors brought
their donkeys loaded down with wares. They had spread
pieces of material on the ground; on them sparkled tin
watches, ceramic crockery, and pieces of mirror, bordered
with gilt trimming, which reflected the frowns of a
stinging sun.

They were: Guiem, son of the blacksmith, sixteen years
old; Toni from Abrés, son of the carter who lived at the
end of the plaza, and whose patio was filled with wheels
propped against the wall and smelled of green wood
(I remember him well: he was blond and taller than the
rest of the boys; he was almost taller than I and he was
only fifteen. When we went to the beach we could see

him from a distance, gathering barnacles from among the rocks, and wearing red trousers.); Antonio, the son of a tenant farmer from Son Lluch, whom we called Antonio of Son Lluch, so as not to confuse him with Toni of Abrés, the carter's son. These three were the principal characters. Then there was Ramón, from the carpenter shop behind the church, who was only thirteen. Guiem, nevertheless, liked to be with him sometimes. It was curious that, at the fatal hour of the siesta, either he went with the whole gang—and then Ramón was one of the followers—or he went alone with Guiem. At that sunlit hour, in the small plaza among the ruins, at the outskirts of the village, next to the canyon that was like a dry river bed (not one river in all of the island, not a single one!), the two of them could be seen together, in the dust, with lancelike green branches. He was only thirteen, but Borja would say: "Guiem likes him around because he knows so much." He was full of malice and wisdom. Sometimes, passing the carpenter shop, I could see him helping his father, among the wood, and he looked at us with his gleaming, small eyes, and smiled as if he were in possession of important secrets (all those things I could not understand). Because of that, Borja said: "They go around with him for what he knows." And the last one (who did not always go with them, but was Ramón's friend) was Sebastián, the cripple, son of the washerwoman of Son Lluch and apprentice to a shoemaker.

And *we* were: Borja, who was the leader, Juan Antonio, the doctor's son, and the two sons of grandmother's

administrator, who lived beyond the Descent, at the beginning of the village, in a house with a large garden and
orchard. They were called León and Carlos, were fourteen and sixteen years old, and were extremely easygoing.
During the winter they studied with the friars. They
went with Borja because their father told them to, but
it seemed to me they saw things in quite a different light
than we. Above all Carlos, the little one, who was a good
student and collected insects in a box. He wore horn-
rimmed glasses and had a receding chin. The two of
them smelled of bread; their fingers were almost always
stained with ink, because their father forced them to
study even during vacations, just as grandmother did
with us. The younger one, Carlos, would say: "I'm going
to be a civil engineer." And Borja would shrug his shoulders. León was more of a loafer and very hypocritical.
The two seemed devout, or at least they pretended they
were, to please their father, and their father was devout
to please grandmother. (Everything went like this on the
island.)

In Guiem's forge there was something poisonous in
the air, in the elongated shadows across the floor, in the
strokes on the anvil, in the puffing of the bellows. Guiem,
with his bare torso and his prominent ribs like the *Young
Simón,* was sweating, his hair stuck to his forehead, his
whole body lit up by the light of the forge. Outside there
were flowers and the well and the odor of mold. And his
mother, the blacksmith's wife, went about with her apron
full of tomatoes, some ripe and others green, and the
bees buzzed among the branches which separated the

garden from the small orchard. And then the kneaded dough, spread out on a tin, covered with herrings and bits of pepper and greens and black olives, which his mother carried to the bakery oven to have baked. It was as if she carried a piece of garden, or a dwarf orchard, where the raw green was most prominent.

Three houses higher up stood the workshop of the carter and Toni. There were no flowers in the carter's patio; there was only a small orchard with some vegetables, and a well. It was usually very dusty and the air was thick with sawdust, like a shower of gold, shimmering in the rays of the sun. Toni from Abrés: I always remember him leaning against the patio wall, under a clear sky which reverberated upon the white stone, with a cutting instrument in his hand, scraping a piece of wood. Leaning up against the wall, barefoot, his eyelashes sprinkled with sawdust and his eyes half-closed, his hair the color of bread crust, dull, without any highlights and falling to both sides, he would say: "All right, if Guiem goes, I'll go." His father was the brother of the carpenter, who was the father of the devilish Ramón. But Toni and his cousin did not get along well together. I never saw them talking to one another.

The days of truce between Borja and Guiem were usually imposed by Borja, not by *them*. And on these days we would share a common cause: to go to the Port, or to Mariné's café to play cards, and spend money gambling or buying things which he kept hidden and said were contraband. Mariné was mysterious with the boys and they always spoke together in half-phrases I did not understand. At times, Mariné won all the money, and he ended up laughing and looking at them in a mocking, snickering manner, while he rolled a cigarette. He always had something prohibited to sell (on one occasion, he even had opium cigarettes) and the boys usually rented the small motorboat from him, in order to go to the Naranjal. The only one to whom Mariné did not rent the boat was Borja, unless Guiem or Toni went along, because he said he was a bad sailor. He would not let him go out alone for all the gold in the world, he used to say. Borja had to depend on the others because he greatly liked going to the Naranjal and spending three whole days there.

During the first part of vacation, they took me out only once, and then we had to come home at night. Grandmother said I was already too much of a woman to go to the Naranjal alone with them and spend three whole nights outside the house. (As if I weren't always alone with them anyway.) But the matter of spending three nights away from home seemed very important. Twice when they went to the Naranjal I accompanied them up to the Port to see them off, without grandmother knowing about it. Then I came back to the house in the *Leontina,* hating the fact that I was a woman. Grandmother never found out. I remember them in the motorboat, barefoot, joyous: the Chink seated, with his knees together, next to the picnic basket, his green glasses glistening. The gulls, like streamers, screamed at the edge of the waves.

That day too I went with them to the Port. (I had first

begged permission: "Grandmother, do let me go with them to the Naranjal." "Never, what a crazy idea, you can never go there! One young girl alone with all those boys! And some of them as bad as Guiem." "But the Chink is going . . ." "And what does that have to do with it?")

There was a balcony in Mariné's café to which only Borja and Guiem were admitted. Borja knew that Guiem and Mariné—who was a short man over fifty, thick in the chest and back—shared secrets in common. They would get together on the large terrace over the sea, where, at twilight, the men from the Port gathered. Mariné would set out glasses on the table. He sold wine, olives, and canned goods. Sometimes, he would serve meals to tourists, if they let him know ahead of time. The people of the Port were very poor; their only livelihood was fishing. They all knew that Mariné and many of those who came to eat on the large terrace over the sea were involved in contraband. Borja used to say: "Guiem knows all the grottoes where the boats put in and dump their bags of goods. Later, someone comes to pick them up." Put this way, it seemed too simple, not something forbidden. There were many grottoes around there. Guiem and Mariné were very good friends; and when I saw them talking together, it became clear to me that Guiem was older, much older, than Borja and I. And it was not exactly his age, but perhaps the way he understood the half-phrases, all of which were lost on us. Even in his smile, Guiem seemed older than Borja, though it was only by one year. Perhaps that was the reason

Borja devised days of truce, when they all went together to the Naranjal. If the weather was good, we sat on coils of rope and sacks on the terrace of Mariné's café. Mariné kept parrots in a number of cages, and he fed them bits of meat on the end of a piece of iron. As soon as they saw us they all began to chatter at the same time, as if they were hurling insults. Mariné lived alone and did the cooking himself. Often, we ate with him, and he served us from a big platter into which we all dipped our own spoons. He could only see out of his right eye, while his left was oddly lurking up under his eyebrow. He always asked after grandmother very respectfully. He hardly spoke a word to the Chink and he laughed when Borja made fun of him. Borja spoke to Mariné about the owner of Son Major. Mariné knew many stories about him, different from the ones we heard from Ton and Antonia, who spoke about him as they might the devil. Mariné was very fond of the owner of Son Major. Borja listened with great attention, and the Chink, in spite of himself, did too. I recall the color of the afternoon, on the terrace over the sea, with the parrots shrieking at us from their cages; and how the light turned blue and gold in the panes of the door. Mariné, sitting between us, said that Jorge of Son Major was a relative of Borja's—he did not mention that he was also my relative—and he looked mockingly at my cousin, who listened to him with his mouth hanging slightly open and his eyes shining.

"And you, Borja, are you going to be like him? Cá, how could you ever be like him! You'd have to be born over again!"

No one spoke to Borja—who smiled without knowing what to answer—in the way Mariné did. I can still see him, kneeling on the sacks, looking vague. The old man held his cigarette in his hand, which was like an enormous crab. He would spit on the ground and laugh. From his bloodshot left eye, a tear was always on the point of falling. And he would say:

"Cá, how could you ever be like him!"

I knew that Borja, even though he smiled sweetly, was quivering with hatred, envy, and rage. And if there was something in the world that he wanted—and he still did not know how much, or at what price—it was that he should be talked about, some day, like Jorge of Son Major. And even if some of them, like Ton himself, spoke to us of Jorge of Son Major in a very different way than Mariné, I think that these opposing versions stimulated Borja even more. (One particular night, in the patio, while the almonds were being shelled, Ton, loquacious as ever, told us things in a low voice and with the secretive air we found so insinuating: "This Jorge of Son Major was crazy, bedeviled. He never wanted to have anything to do with the people around here, nor did he have one single friend in this village, or in his class. He went looking for friends in other places, at sea. And what friends he found—they all had something of the pirate about them! Mariné signed on the *Delfín;* he went with Don Jorge to the pagan lands . . . Yes, Don Jorge was mad, absolutely mad; or rather, perhaps, it was as if a devil had taken possession of his body. His father spoiled him, that's it. He could only see things through his eyes. And the poor old man died alone, in Son Major, calling for him, calling out for him . . . while his son wandered about those accursed islands like a wild man. When he came back, the old man was already buried, and he didn't even go into mourning, or pay to have some funeral services said, as was only right . . . Ay, no! He was much worse. He filled the house with bad people, and they said that in that house, with the devil's wind blowing through it, they carried on some ghastly bacchanals. And they say that one night the devil was seen to come in, wrapped in his cape and wearing black glasses, and horrible guffaws were heard along the cliff. No one wanted to get near the *Delfín.* It was bewitched. The people from the Port said that it glowed infernally at night . . . God knows what was going on in there! And here, a woman whose name I won't mention, a very important woman in the city, left her husband to go off with him. Nothing more was ever heard about her; it was as if she had been swallowed up by hell. Women were bewitched by him: they went crazy over him and ended up by going off with that devil. The whole island was outraged. And as for wives . . . at least four of them. One of them was not of the Christian race; her skin was dark, and she spoke something no one understood. He didn't spend a month here even: he always lived on the *Delfín,* as on a phantom boat, without working, just throwing money away on his crazy whims. He went on losing it all, flinging away his money in the worst way . . . But, children, time is cruel. Time flies for all of us. There he is now: a sick old man, without a single friend . . . The children are afraid of him because their mothers tell them: *If you're not good the man from Son Major will carry you off.* It's the hand of God. Everything in life passes away, children, everything.")

And then Mariné:

"Now he doesn't let himself be seen, he never goes out. He's dying."

He became pensive and added:

"Some day I'll go see him. He remembers me: I was one of his sailors. If someone from those days goes to visit him, he serves him good wine. He's a gentleman; he doesn't look down on people who served him. Yes, he's a gentleman. There are few of his kind left."

The Chink said:

"In the old days, Doña Práxedes was a good friend of his."

"In the old days! . . . Now he doesn't want to have anything to do with his relatives. Some day I'll go and see him, yes sir . . . We sailed a good bit together. We went to the islands," and suddenly, his red, stubby hand with its pawlike fingers pointed out to sea. And, in the distance, there was a bright spot which made a knot in one's throat just to look at it. "And now, there he is, locked up in that house. Bah! With that disgusting Sanamo, taking advantage of the old days aboard the *Delfín,* and the memories of that poor man! Yes, stirring up memories in him with his rotten guitar, to keep from getting thrown out in the street: he was always a traitor and nothing more! The last of the *Delfín,* the very last!"

In a corner, Guiem laughed gloomily:

"Yes, they know Don Jorge everywhere! Absolutely everywhere!"

Mariné and Guiem smiled mysteriously. Borja said in a screechy voice:

"We have the same last name. The family used to get on very well: the Chink's right. My grandmother was a good friend of his . . . And no one has finished with anyone, really."

"No one, child, no one." Mariné transferred his cigarette butt from one side of his mouth to the other. "You'll be heir, you can bet on that!"

Guiem was crushing ants with his foot. (Ants were everywhere on the island. There were roads and roads of ants through the whole island; miniature, tiny tunnels drilled through it, like an infinity of hollow veins; the ants coming and going all the time.) Mariné put a sieve-like ladle in the earthen jar of black olives and dished them out, dripping, onto the small plate:

"You'll go to see him, won't you?"

The Chink put his hand on Borja's shoulder, a strange hand at that moment: yellow, dry. It was not a friendly hand, but it nevertheless wanted or asked for something. Borja stayed still, with his fixed smile which I knew so well:

"Yes. Certainly I'll go see him one of these days. He's an uncle of mine."

"Something like that, something like that," laughed Mariné. "Well, when you go to see him, talk to him about me, about the old days. Look, he had gold piled up in a cabinet. Rolls and rolls of gold coins! Then he would say: 'Take it, Mariné, you're a good fellow.' I served him well, but not on a steady salary, no!"

Again, Guiem and Mariné looked into each others' eyes and laughed deep down. How old and astute Guiem seemed then, with his evil black eyes! Borja also forced a laugh. The wine Mariné sold was very bad and it left our teeth and lips dark. Sometimes we bought a kind of strong spirits that made us very happy.

"Ay, he went around all the islands," he dreamed on, with his right eye shining like grandmother's solitaire. "It was a bad thing when he sold his boat . . . Even if there are some who say he didn't sell it, but burned it up. I don't know what he did with the *Delfín*. And all of us loved it! The truth is that I thought: 'Has the owner of Son Major gotten rid of the *Delfín?*' Then he must be in a very bad way."

"He's not sick now," said the Chink. "I saw him the other day behind the iron gate of his garden watering his flowers."

"Badly off, badly off," muttered Mariné. And his eye lost itself definitively in his snarled eyebrow.

Coming back on the *Leontina,* when they had gone off to the Naranjal, I thought over all this. I reached the pier, climbed the Descent, bitter at having seen them go off, and prey to a strange dreaminess that those conversations produced in me. I entered the patio of the house through the small door and went up silently, so grandmother might not find out about my escapade to the Port, to wash and change my clothes for dinner. Afterwards, grandmother asked me:

"Where have you been?"

"Studying."

Grandmother looked at my fingers to see if they were still stained with ink. She neared her big nose to my mouth to find out if I had smoked. (Before coming in I chewed a mint candy furiously, one of those which Mariné kept in tall cans, with the trademark of some bouillon cubes.)

I asked Antonia:

"What is the owner of Son Major like? Is it true he had the devil in his house?"

She turned down my bedclothes and ran her hand along the folded part of the sheet, stretching it out. She turned and said:

"That gentleman is already very old. He was a great young man, a bit odd . . . Well, he was a gentleman, that he was, very generous and a bit mad. Around here, the people couldn't understand him . . . He amused himself in his own way, in a scandalous manner: here, no one does things like that. He was . . . How could I say it? He lashed out at everything, like the wind! He squandered his fortune. It was scandalous."

"He still has a lot of money! A cabinet full of gold coin."

"Bah. And what's that for him? That's nothing," she answered.

And as she said this, she thickened her lips scornfully. (I do not know why the thought of that photograph taken of her and Lauro when he was still small, and stuck now in the angle of the mirror, came to me.) Antonia laughed briefly, and lowering her voice even more, she added, as if for herself alone:

"He had humor still, still . . . giving José Taronjí and Malene those lands, precisely in the middle of the Descent, in the middle of your grandmother's lands . . . That made Doña Práxedes pretty furious."

(Under the sky which darkened little by little, on the way back home in the *Leontina,* I thought about those things. I looked at my suntanned legs stretched out, and I said to myself that perhaps it was true what they told us. But in life, it seemed to me, there was something too real. I knew—because it was always being repeated to me—that the world was big and bad. And it scared me to think that it could be even more terrifying than I imagined. And I looked at the earth, and I told myself that we lived on top of the dead; that the stony island, with its enormous flowers and trees, was a mass formed by the piling up of corpses, corpses upon corpses. Mariné said once that Jorge of Son Major had caused many deaths, that he was cruel, but that there was no one in the world as generous or worthy. What deaths was he talking about? What cruelties? At the end of the Descent stood the well, next to the stone stairway where I had pushed Juan Antonio away one afternoon. The well had a big dragon head with an open mouth, covered with moss. And there was a very deep echo when something fell to the bottom. Even the rolling of the chain had a horrifying echo. And I used to bend my head over the darkness of the well, down toward the water. It was like smelling the dark heart of the earth.)

"Have you seen Saint George in the stained-glass window?" Mariné said that day. "Don Jorge of Son Major was like that."

Crossed by the sun in Santa María, surrounded by transparent reds like goblets of ruby wine, Saint George shone with golden crown, plate armor, and long green sword.

"Like a Saint George. And they say that the painter took an ancestor of his for a model."

"What a lie!" said the Chink, who after taking off his glasses covered his eyes. "Please be quiet and leave those lovely stained-glass windows alone . . ."

(I always thought that the Martyrs of the stained-glass windows were, for the Chink, something like vengeful brothers who looked at us from on high, shining in the obscurity of Santa María, where frightened lizards and rats scooted about like papers blown by the wind. And the sun, there outside, lay in ambush like a lion.)

Mariné banged his fist down on the table and the black olives jumped in the tiny plate. Guiem's coarse laugh could be heard and Mariné barked:

"Like Saint George, I said, he's like Saint George, and the vermin can shut up! Yes, sir; as handsome and fat as Saint George . . . and loaded down with souvenirs and talismans and rosaries of amber. I've seen them. Look," Mariné half-opened his smelly shirt and showed

us a rare silver coin with a sign on it. "He gave it to
me . . . He was different, he was head and shoulders
above everybody else. They told him: 'Why don't you
leave that damned boat, why don't you stop making those
voyages which are eating away your health and money,
and live like other men. Go to the city, to the Continent,
enjoy yourself like others, don't waste your life with
these things!' But he would answer: 'No, I belong to
another race.' It's true, he was like the wind. Like a God,
I swear."

Mariné crossed two fingers and kissed them. A smack-
ing noise sounded. Without any relevance, the Chink
said:

"The kiss of Judas."

Mariné was irritated. He pulled out his knife and put
it on his chest. The Chink backed up against the wall.
The wind blew in his face, and he closed his eyes because
he had not put on his glasses, which he held in one raised
and trembling hand.

"Of what God are you a prophet, renegade?"
screamed Mariné, his face red with fury. "Of what God?
You don't believe in anything. They threw you out of
there as an unbeliever. You only believe in your piggish
belly," and with the point of his knife he pointed out
the Chink's black and sunken stomach—beneath brown
buttons—palpitating with fear. "You don't believe in
anything but your piggish guts! What is it that you're
going to teach these innocents?"

He was referring to us. Then he spit, and said:

"It's death you teach them! Dead men, nothing more.

You don't know anything besides death . . . Go on, renegade, Judas. Go call the Taronjís, so they can come and get me."

Mariné moved away. Borja got up in one jump and went for more wine.

"Eh, eh!" Mariné screamed to him.

Borja, ostentatiously, showed him his money. He carried it rolled up and held together with a rubber band in his right-hand pocket. He raised the edge of his sweater, and along the waist of his pants the butt of grandfather's old revolver stuck out. Mariné's humor changed suddenly, and he began to laugh in such a way that his face turned purple and he looked as if he were going to burst.

He sold us contraband tobacco and rum. And he gave Guiem and Borja something mysterious that they didn't let me see.

"You no, pretty, not you," my cousin said, moving away from me.

His lips and eyes were brilliant and it seemed to me that the wine had gone to everybody's head.

Furious, I had to return alone in the *Leontina*. They, the rotters, all jumped aboard Mariné's motorboat. They let out screams, unwound ropes, and climbed up over the prow. The sun beat down against their backs: they were like the stained-glass figures in Santa María, black and red against the sky.

Even the wind hurt me and Mariné told me:

"Climb aboard the boat, little one. And go on, go on home."

Then, I knew it already: two or three days, or maybe only a single day of truce.

2

If Borja could count on the carbine and grandfather's old revolver, and Juan Antonio on the knife, and the administrator's children on the whips, Guiem and his gang had hooks from the butcher shop for "war" days. The shop was at the end of a high street. Once I saw a lamb's head hanging at the door; its eye, brutal, intense, almost exasperated, protruded from between blue veins. Guiem and his gang stole the hooks one by one, and hid them under their shirts. When we encountered them in the small plaza of the Jews, they brandished them with great braggadocio. Hidden between the rocks, they threw stones at us, but not so as to "hit," since they first had to "provoke" us. Then they went toward the woods. They screamed at the Chink:

"Judas, Judas, Judas!"

Borja, Juan Antonio, or the administrator's children had to go after them. They started their atrocious fights between the trees, pursuing one another cruelly. My cousin, with the revolver or carbine, kept them at a distance. It was a silent, merciless war, whose sense was beyond my comprehension, yet it worried me, not because of the damage they could cause each other, but rather because I sensed something dark in it, something which unnerved me. Once they wounded Juan Antonio with a hook. I remember the blood running down, between the black hairs on his leg, and his lips pressed tightly together so as not to cry. His only concern was that his father should not find out. Borja took care of him by tying a handkerchief soaked in sea water tightly around his leg. Sometimes, Borja, too, emerged from the battle with some scratch or other: but he was as cautious and slippery as an eel, and his carbine terrorized Guiem, who would scream at him:

"No fair using the carbine! It's no fair!"

The small plaza of the Jews, where Guiem's gang began their maneuvers to get us going by lighting bonfires, was in an old quarter of town and had been destroyed many years ago by a fire. Only some scorched, ruined porticos and two houses about to cave in remained, at the side of the road climbing up to the charcoal burners' woods. The land came to an abrupt end, as if sheared off clean at the high wall of the cliff. To the right lay the Descent, and the whiteness of Malene Taronjí's house. The dazzling sea spread out below. It was the same sea I saw in my atlas, but immense and alive, trembling with a great green vertigo, marked with thicker zones and spots, fringed with gulls quivering like flags perched off the coast. From above, from the plaza, where Jews were once burned alive, the sea appeared full of terror, of unease: it was like a round blue menace, blending into the wind and sky, where shining universes or wandering echoes of fear would lose themselves. From above, the only possibility seemed to be to roll down and down. And life seemed something hideous and far away.

Against grandmother's heavy face, against Monsignor Mayol's handsome features, against the impenetrable waiting of Aunt Emilia, and against the hard heart which lodged behind the pleats in Antonia's dress I had built my own island. We, Borja and I, were clear about one thing: we were alone. Often, when night had fallen, we would pound on the wall three times. He would jump out of his bed, and I out of mine. As silently as goblins we would cross through hallways and bedrooms and meet on the loggia.

The sky glittered between the arches, and mysterious and fugitive sparks dropped out of the darkness of the caissoned ceiling. "I couldn't sleep." "I couldn't either." We threw ourselves face downward on the floor so that we would not be seen from the windows, and smoked in silence. I carried my black doll, which nobody knew about, worn-out and dirty and dressed as a harlequin, under my pajamas, next to my skin. I took out the sticky, saliva-covered candy from under my tongue and threw it away. My mouth smelled of mint, and he would say: "What are you chewing, gum or candy?" I was ashamed of either of the two things and I answered: "It's the tooth-paste that smells like that." And we went on smoking Aunt Emilia's *Murattis,* silently. At times he would ob-serve: "When will all this end! Who do you think will win the war? It seems to me that our side, because they're Catholics and believe in God, is bound to win." "I don't know who'll win; no one ever knows that." Often, he would talk about things past: "You know, we used to have a very pretty house there. I went to school . . ."

He spoke of his land and his friends, and I listened without understanding very well. But I liked the tone of his voice. I gazed toward the arches and sky and thought: "Mauricia." (The orchard, my father's house, the woods and the river, bordered with poplars. The river, with its green, still backwaters, like large eyes in the earth!) We were so defenseless, living under so much pressure, so—oh, yes—so far from them: from Uncle Álvaro's portrait, the Taronjís, the recollection of my father, Antonia, the Chink . . . How foreign is the race of adults, the race of men and women! How foreign and absurd we were! How outside of the world and even of time. We were no longer children. We suddenly did not know what we were. And in this way, without knowing why, face downward on the floor, we did not dare come close to one another. He put his hand on top of mine and only our heads touched. Sometimes I was aware of the curls on his forehead, or the cold tip of his nose. And he would say, between puffs of smoke: "When will all this end . . . !" It is certainly true that neither of us was sure what he was referring to: if it were the war, the island, or our very age. Sometimes, a sudden light would surge from a bedroom, and a yellow square of it fall upon us. And we felt a sudden shame when we thought of someone approaching, seeing us and asking: "What are you doing here?" What would we answer? Against all of them, and their hard or indifferent words, even against Borja, and Guiem, and Juan Antonio, and against the absence of my parents, I had my island: that corner of the wardrobe where lived, under my handkerchiefs, socks, and atlas, my small black doll. Between white handkerchiefs and green fields and seas of blue paper, with cities like tiny pinheads, my small Gorogó lived hidden from the brutal curiosity of the outside world. And in the glossy atlas—as I stood with half my body inside the wardrobe closet, hidden in the darkness, smelling the mahogany and starch—I could glance over captivating countries: the Greek islands to which Jorge of Son Major sailed in his now-vanished *Delfín,* escaping, perhaps (like me?), from men and women, from the awful world he so much feared. I went on looking at my atlas; there was Uncle Álvaro's war also, the conquered cities ("It has fallen, it has fallen." *"Te Deum . . ."*). The war in which my father was lost, shipwrecked, sunk, because of his bad ideas. The war, there on the map, in the still-unconquered zones, dragged him down like a swamp. And what was left of him? (Oh yes, tiny Peter Pan, Never-Never Land, *The Misfortunes of Sophie . . .* And his? No, no. He surely knew nothing of Never-Never Land.) And the recollection—there with my head stuck inside the wardrobe closet, bent forward from my waist, and the satiny rustle of the atlas's pages fluttering in a kind of restrained conversation—the memory of him scarcely reached me, except perhaps in the echo of his voice crying out: *"Matia, Matia, haven't you anything to say to me? It's papa . . ."* (The small telephone station in the village: I on tiptoe, the black instrument brought quiveringly close to my cheek, and a lump in my throat.) Whom was I talking to, with whom? With the person who had left a marvelous crystal ball which snowed inside in a drawer in the house? (*"It belonged to your father: he used to love to make it snow when he was a boy . . ."*). The word "father" was there, enclosed in that white crystal ball, like a monstrous drop of rain which I brought close to my right eye—the left one stayed closed—and, turning the ball upside down, it would snow. Yes, only that voice: *"Haven't you anything to say to me?"* And then, the other voice, Mauricia's, with the afternoon mail delivery: *"Look what your papa sent you . . ."*

(Inside the wardrobe closet lay my small baggage of memories: the black, twisted telephone wire echoing his voice, like a surprising stream of resounding blood. The apples in the attic, the Island of Never-Never Land, and its spring cleanings) . . . But we lived on another island. Yes, on this island we seemed lost, surrounded by the terrible blue of the sea, and, above all, by silence. Boats did not sail past our coasts, nothing was heard, or seen: nothing but the breathing of the sea. There, on the loggia, I clutched my small Negrito, who had been mine for as long as I could remember. It was this doll I had taken with me to Our Lady of the Angels, the one the assistant headmistress tried to throw in the rubbish, so that I had kicked her and been expelled. This was the doll I sometimes called Gorogó—and it was for him that I drew miniature cities in the corners and margins of my books, invented at the point of my pen, with winding spiral staircases, sharpened cupolas, bell towers, and asymmetrical nights—and whom at other times I simply called Negrito, and who was only an unfortunate boy who cleaned chimneys in a very far-off city in a Hans Christian Andersen story.

Turned against everyone, when I returned in the *Leontina*—banished for being a girl (not even a woman, not even that) from the excursion to the Naranjal—against all of them, I went up to my room, and took my small Negrito out from under the handkerchiefs and socks, stared into his tiny face and asked myself why I could no longer love him.

3

Borja was a thief. I do not know how he acquired this vice, or if he had just been born with it. The fact was that Borja could not think of life without his continual and almost systematic thefts, especially of money. He stole from his mother and grandmother skillfully, and he took a special pleasure in the danger, the fear of being discovered. It is obvious that their enormous confidence in him, their belief in his innocence and his supposed nobility made thieving easy for him. He usually stole things from his mother's room. Aunt Emilia was careless and she often left money scattered on the dresser or some other piece of furniture, and then she would complain mournfully:

"Money goes so fast, it slips right through your fingers, I don't understand how . . ."

To steal from grandmother was much more exciting. She usually kept her money in a small metal box, which would reflect misshapen versions of our faces and become steamed up with our breathing. She had it on a shelf in her wardrobe, and on top of it would always put—as if she wanted to protect it—her missal and the case containing her Rosary of Indulgences, brought back from a trip to Lourdes. To one side, like a sentinel, she placed a crystal bottle full of miracle-making water, from which she drank a swallow now and then. The bottle was in the shape of the Virgin, and the crown unscrewed like a stopper. Borja had to climb up on a chair—the shelf was too high for him, as he was short—and maneuver for a long time. First to put the Bottle-Image to one side, then to move the missal and case, and finally, to turn the key in the box, open it and take out the money. The bills were generally folded over to form tiny books, and he concentrated on taking them out carefully and putting them back in their place in such a way that she would not notice anything. In the hallway, next to the carillon clock, I performed guard duty, watching over the staircase for the sound of the beast's footsteps. When I stood guard, I got a cut of the booty. A large part of it was invested in cigarettes from Mariné and in mint candies to dissipate traces of cigarette odor.

Grandmother used to thrust her long bony finger into my mouth, like a hook:

"At your age you should no longer eat candy, aren't you ashamed? Besides, you'll spoil your teeth."

I recall that one of the most humiliating things of those days was grandmother's constant preoccupation with my possible future beauty: with a hypothetical beauty that I ought to acquire, come what may.

"It's the only thing a woman has if she doesn't have money."

Beauty, then, was the only worthwhile thing one could count on in life. However, my beauty was still somewhat nebulous and far off, and my appearance left a good deal to be desired, to grandmother's way of thinking. To begin with, she found me outrageously tall and skinny. Aunt Emilia, she would say, had not been beautiful, but she had been rich and she married Uncle Álvaro (a man apparently both important and wealthy). My mother had been very good-looking, and rich, but she allowed herself to be carried away by the ridiculous sentiments of a romantic girl, and she paid a high price for her choice. My father, grandmother said, was an unprincipled man, obsessed by distorted ideas, in the cultivation of which he squandered my mother's money and consequently ruined their family life. "Such men should never marry. They sow evil wherever they go." Fortunately, according to her, that marriage did not last long: my mother died before things took a scandalous turn. In sum, beauty and money, double-edged weapons, had both to be looked out for.

Grandmother worried a great deal about my teeth—too big and too far apart—and my eyes ("Don't look out of the corner of your eye like that." "Don't squint." "Good God, this child is going to have a cast in her right eye!"). My hair, hopelessly straight, bothered her, and my legs concerned her too:

"You're so thin . . . Well, I guess it's only your age. We'll have to wait until you change, little by little. In a couple of years from now we probably won't recognize you. But I'm afraid you look too much like your father."

Seated in her rocking chair, scrutinizing me with her round owl eyes, she would make me walk about and sit down; she would examine my eyes and hands. (She reminded me of the villagers on market days, when they bought a mule.) She criticized my suntanned skin and the freckles which were appearing around my nose because of the sun.

"Always in the sun, like a little scamp! Good God, what a mess: a big mouth, eyes far apart . . . Now, don't make your eyes tiny! You'll get crow's feet. Pull back your shoulders, your head . . . Now, bite your lips a bit, wet them . . ."

I could not help hating her then. I wanted her to drop down dead, suddenly, right then and there, with her feet up in the air like a bird. She would run her tiny bamboo cane up and down my back to straighten it and hit me on my knees and shoulders.

"Some day you'll thank me for all this . . . Now you can go."

Behind that "now you can go" was a recital of Latin declensions, Corneille translation, the reading aloud of the *Child of the Secret,* the tiny Guido de Fontagalland —reading it out loud so that she need not tire her vision and could listen, or pretend to listen, seated in her rocking chair next to the window. Then, at the window, she would turn her opera glasses on her monstrous toy, the Descent, and probe it. Close to her hand was the snuff box and the slowly sliding bamboo cane.

I preferred punishment to all that. Suddenly I would run away, without paying any attention to her voice:

"Matia! Matia! Come back at once!"

Even if Borja was not there, I would go down the Descent, as far as the sea, and sit down ruefully between the pitas. I would prowl around like a miserable dog, beyond the walls of the Descent, with my shadow behind me. I would flee toward some place, far away, where I could be alone.

"Now you can go . . ."

I left the room, looking back over my shoulder, since this gesture particularly irritated her. On grandmother's hooked finger stayed the remains of my candy, which she carefully cleaned off with her handkerchief.

Then, if Borja was not there (traitor, traitor, he had gone off to the Naranjal, knowing that I could not go along; he had gone off, and he knew I had to stay at home, feigning indifference, swallowing my humiliation as I leaned against the wall, with my legs crossed, biting anything so no one would notice I was holding back tears), if Borja was not there I remained in grandmother's clutches, along with stupid Aunt Emilia who smoked in her room and drank brandy on the sly (ah, her pinky little eyes), waiting, waiting, waiting, with her big white belly, for ferocious Uncle Álvaro's return. Uncle Álvaro, who, according to Borja, ordered men shot as he entered their villages, and whom Borja had never given a kiss or looked straight in the eye, and who punished him for whole days with bread and water if he brought home low grades from the School of Christ the King. Uncle Álvaro. All that remained of him was a box of Havana cigars, which I put close to my nose and sniffed with my eyes closed; a belt with silver buckles; and some harnesses and a riding saddle, all covered with dust, in the patio. And those whips, which hung on the wall, made me tremble just to look at them.

"They were grandfather's."

"And Uncle Álvaro's?"

"Well . . . he used them too, when he came here."

(Uncle Álvaro was not a native of the island. Borja would always say: "We are Navarrese." And they had a very large house with a patio and horse stables in that part of the country. "That really was nice," Borja said, sighing. "But grandmother loves you very much, Borja. It's different with me. You're going to inherit this house. . . .") And those whips hung next to the kitchen window, where I climbed and heard Ton commenting: "Those men were like animals . . . she'll defend me." Those whips, how could they belong to anyone but Uncle Álvaro, with his face like the edge of a knife, and his mouth twisted by a scar? Borja looked like him; and yet, how could he be so soft and handsome at the same time? And Borja sometimes had the same way of looking, of twisting his mouth into an expression resembling a wicked cutting edge.

The last day Borja was at the Naranjal, grandmother said, after eating:

"I'm going to rest. Matia, go upstairs for a while and lie down. It's good for you to rest after meals; Juan Antonio's father said so."

For a week or so, this detestable custom had been established because of Juan Antonio's father. The siesta hour, when everyone was resting, was my favorite time of day. I recall the heat. The windows were open and not even the lightest breeze stirred the curtains. In the garden, a shining dust floated over the trees, among the buzzing of the insects. Aunt Emilia got up, and said:

"I'm going up to write some letters."

She always had letters to write, a terrible bundle of letters, which I supposed she sent to the front. Sometimes she said:

"Come with me, Matia."

And that afternoon too, she said it. I hated to go up with her, but I did not dare refuse. Aunt Emilia's room was very big, with an adjoining sitting room. The enormous double bed, the small pink upholstered armchairs, the heavy wardrobe closet, the dressing table, the chest of drawers, the flowing curtains, and the sun were all part of the room. The sun suddenly blazed like a thousand bees buzzing on the balcony. The sun stuck to the white, transparent material, and shed its brilliance onto the bed, with its white cushions which smelled of apples and starch.

Aunt Emilia took off her dress, and "freshened up," as she said, by putting on a hideous, pale green robe, wrinkled and saturated with an old perfume which was sickening, like everything else in that room. There

was something about that room which I could not
fathom; something trapped and enclosed by the curtains
which were pulled together so that the fury of the sun
should not strike us at that oppressive and threatening
hour; something sweetish and decaying at the same time.
I unwillingly took off my sandals and clothes (the eternal
white blouse and the ghastly box-pleated skirt), and
Aunt Emilia braided my hair, and wound it around the
top of my head.

"Go on now, lie down and try to sleep. No stories,
candies, or chewing gum. You might swallow the gum."

I threw myself down on the bed, hiding my bad humor
and breathing in that unpleasant perfume: besides, some
jasmines on the dressing table gave off their heavy
fragrance. Lying like that, open-eyed and gazing at the
ceiling, I heard the crickets chirping in the Descent.
The room was thick and obscene, like Aunt Emilia's big
stomach and breasts. I saw the way she went to the wardrobe closet and poured herself some brandy in a very
lovely, ruby-colored glass. I pretended to close my eyes,
but I looked at her between my eyelids. She drank the
brandy down in one swallow and then went to the sink,
turned the faucet—all the pipes began to groan, to blow,
as if they were mumbling curses—and rinsed the glass.
Afterwards, she lit a cigarette and fell into an armchair
and leafed through the magazines that Monsignor Mayol
usually lent her, and which she never read. Suddenly,
there was something odd in that room. It was as if someone had hung the whips and harnesses from the patio
on the bedroom wall. Something brutal and cruel cut

through the room and ripped its calmness in two (perhaps the memory of Uncle Álvaro), because of something she said.

"Your uncle . . ."

Half-reclining in her armchair, she stretched her arm out toward the balcony and lifted the curtain, and a vivid ray of sun poured through, like a golden sword. I watched her spongy profile, the rings under her eyes, and I said to myself: "What a pity! She's going to seed." And through my confused imagination galloped strange ideas, of Uncle Álvaro and her; ideas incited by some of Juan Antonio's and Borja's conversations. Things I pretended to understand completely, but which were still vague and enigmatic. I felt something like fear then, and I curled up in a corner, to one side of the bed. Because there, to the right—I can still see them—lay the cushions with their embroidered slip covers, smelling as if they had just been ironed, and I said to myself: "That pillow is Uncle Álvaro's, that's his place. Aunt Emilia is forever waiting for him." And something that was not exactly fear ran down my spine. It was more like a strange embarrassment, as I recalled the things Borja and Juan Antonio would tell about men and women. And I said to myself: "No, they're probably just so many more lies." And I wanted death also to be a lie. I closed my eyes. Aunt Emilia kept her letters in a wooden box, and she took them out, one by one, and re-read them; it seemed to me that the box gave off an intrusive odor of cedar and leather which belonged to Uncle Álvaro. And I felt a stranger in that world. I had taken Gorogó with me, and had him hidden next to my chest, under my slip. At that moment Aunt Emilia said:

"What are you hiding there?"

"Nothing!"

She came up to me and managed to grab him from me, even though I had thrown myself face down on the bed to protect him. She turned him over in her hands. I stayed buried in the pillow, so that she would not see how red I had blushed (I even felt my ears burning). Instead of mocking me, she said:

"Ah, it's a doll! . . . Yes, I also slept with a doll, practically up until the night before my wedding."

I lifted my head to look at her, and I saw her smiling. I took the doll out of her hands to put it under my pillow, thinking: "It's not that. I don't sleep with my arms around Gorogó any more. I never really slept with him, only with a bear named Celín. This one is for other things: for traveling and for listening to my troubles. It's not a doll for loving, stupid." But she went on:

"You're always asking me for cigarettes, and now it turns out you still play with dolls."

She put her hand to my head and mussed my bangs. She went up to the dresser and took out a *Muratti* from a little box (on which a winter garden was drawn, with pots filled with date palms, and a man dressed in a tuxedo, his legs crossed, smoking, all very commonplace). She put it between my lips, smiling. She lit it herself and said:

"Your mother and I were very fond of each other,

Matia. Come on now, be a good girl: smoke this cigarette.
You see how understanding I am. But then close your
eyes and try to sleep."

She looked at her tiny wristwatch and added:

"I'll give you ten minutes to smoke. But then rest,
even if it's only for half an hour. Afterwards, if you
don't make any noise going down the stairs, I promise
I'll let you leave."

She poured herself another shot of brandy, and fell
into the armchair with her letters. The jasmines were
turning yellow, and on the dresser, in the bell jar, flowers
and more flowers were piled up around the images of
San Bruno and Santa Catalina.

Aunt Emilia would fall asleep in the folding chair,
which was faded by the sun because it was used in the
garden on spring days. She still had not finished her
cigarette, and was sleeping, collapsed in the chair. I recall the heat—it was the end of August—and that a fly
buzzed, trapped between the curtain and the glass. The
odor of sun lit up the walls, drawing a heavy perfume
from the brilliant mahogany of the dresser, and a spicy
odor from the saints and flowers, which mixed with
Aunt Emilia's powder and a subtle aroma of brandy.
I could taste the sweetish, exotic flavor of the Turkish
cigarette on my tongue and the roof of my mouth, and
between my lips was the glitter of the gold filter that I
scarcely dared hold there, for I was frightened of smoking
in front of her. I stood up slowly, so as not to startle
her. She was stretched out, her white, massive arm in

the pink and gold shadows of the room. In the green crystal ashtray, the cigarette butt was burning out. And the fly, still imprisoned between the folds of the curtain and the glass, could not escape.

I stood up slowly, leaning over to look at her. It was like leaning over a well. It was as if suddenly Aunt Emilia had decided to tell me all the secrets of a grownup, and I did not know where to hide my amazed and shame-covered face. To see her in that state, abandoned, her mouth hanging open, sunken into sadness with her eyes closed (one more closed than the other, which showed a shiny glassiness between her right eyelid and cheek), overwhelmed me. Her flesh bulged from her robe, and I contemplated her sprawling legs, with her skirt hoisted to the right, and her bare foot ("Why does she polish her toenails?"). I looked at my own dark, skinny, scratched legs, my little saint's feet—like Borja's —with the nails cut square (one turning blue and split because of a blow, and hurting if I pressed on it with my toe) and I said to myself: "I'm going to polish my toenails too." But how far away all that was! It would be in another life, almost in another world, when I would feel the same as Aunt Emilia, with her *Murattis* and her letters, and her blank empty waiting, sunken into stupor, searching for sad company in the ruby-colored glass full of brandy (jealously hidden in her wardrobe) without a real thought about the war. Only that he might win, I thought, and return to see her toenails so neatly polished. "He won't like her so fat." But

I was ashamed of thinking that. I slid along the floor, trying not to make noise, nor move the loud pages of the magazines and newspapers scattered about her. I stepped onto the rug with great care and looked for my sandals. Then I stepped over the legs of the defenseless woman who was so immodestly revealing the dark things of grown-up people to me. I went up to the chest of drawers, and picked up the ruby-colored glass. Holding it up, I looked at myself in the mirror, at my skinny, sunburnt shoulders where the white straps stood out against my skin, and locks of hair streamed from the braids so badly tied by Aunt Emilia, the gold of the sun forming a halo. The reddish locks of hair reminded me of something: "Against the light I seem to be a red-head like Manuel, and everyone thinks of me as black-haired." To show them to myself, I bared my teeth, which grandmother feared I would ruin with sweets and aromatic mint candies: "I'm not a woman. Oh, no, I'm not a woman," and I felt unburdened, as if a weight had been lifted from me, but my knees shook. I stuck my tongue inside the red glass, furiously. (But damn her, the wretch, how well she had rinsed it.)

The most difficult part—as when Borja stole money from grandmother's box—was opening the door silently. To do that, Borja and I had learned to grease the door hinges of the wild beasts' rooms with a rooster feather soaked in oil.

Gorogó had fallen pathetically onto the rug, with his arms crossed and his black face against the floor. I picked

him up and put him against my breast again, entangling
his head in the chain from which my medal hung. I
quickly gathered up my clothes, went into the little adjoining sitting room and got dressed. With my sandals
still in my hand, I went out. At the end of the corridor,
the tic-toc of the carillon clock broke the silence. My
shadow pursued me, elongated, as far as the staircase. I
sat down on the first step and slipped on my sandals.
It was so hot that I seemed to be breathing inside the
haze of a dream. (And it is absolutely true that for a
long time—and even now, this very minute—I remembered that afternoon as if it lay at the bottom of a large
goblet, all noise deadened. And in that suffocating silence
I only heard the voices and words of Manuel's and my
first conversation. Only my own voice and Manuel's
mixed. And the tiny, penetrating eyes of the green lizard
—so close to our heads, like a monster—looking at us
from between the grasses, as the two of us were
stretched out on the ground of the Descent.)

As I walked out onto the patio, the sun stirred up a
white fury on the walls, and under the arches the shadows
turned into a damp and dense steam. I stood for a moment next to Ton's gear, and I heard Lorenza's voice:
"How can we turn him down?"
And then Antonia:
"Give it to him and don't let anybody find out . . .
Don't tell anyone where you got it, not even your
mother."

Then the two of them left, Manuel behind Lorenza. They turned the corner. Lorenza carried a key in her hand and they went around the yellow edge of the house.

"Where are they going, Antonia? What did Manuel want?"

"Drinking water . . . Somebody killed their dog and threw it in the well."

"Who?"

She shrugged her shoulders and kept on sewing, bent over her work.

"Who knows?"

I turned my eyes away from her puckered mouth, full of pins. I followed Lorenza's steps. They led to the well in the orchard, where the Descent began.

I leaned against one of the olive trees, looking at them. From down below, the green radiance of the sea mounted between the pitas. The trees, in silhouette, seemed black. Manuel was bent over the well, and Lorenza dropped in the pail. I heard the sound of water. It was a lovely noise, like cold silver in the burning silence. "They've thrown a dead dog in." I looked at my feet. Absently, I drew patterns in the earth with the edge of my sandal. "It'll smell hideously. They can't drink it now, and they've come to ask for water."

"You don't know who did it?" Lorenza asked in her dialect.

He did not answer; he was leaning over the mouth of the well. His dark arms glistened as he raised the rope. The stone dragon—the Chink said it was twelfth-century—seemed to laugh amid the moss.

"Take what you want," Lorenza said in a low voice. "But don't let them see you, don't tell anybody anything . . ."

She turned around and walked off. I stood quietly, sheltered by the olive tree. Manuel raised the water from the well and poured it into his pitcher. It was a large, green-enameled pitcher. "A dead dog is something awful," I said to myself, "something no one can stand."

4

Perhaps what disconcerted me was that he was not furious. Upon hearing my steps he raised his head, and I remember—as clearly as if it were happening right now at my side—the clanking of the pulley, and the dark dankness which rose from the well. It was a warm dankness like the breath of the earth. I said: "Is the water very cold?" or something similar. It was perhaps even something still more banal, but I managed to get him to turn his head and look at me. I knew the sun-tanned back of his neck from having seen him bent over in the orchard. When he turned his face toward me, I thought: "He's never looked at me before." The afternoon he went off in the boat, he did not look at us, neither Borja nor me. (Suddenly the odor of the mayor's patio on the morning they returned from burying José Taronjí came to me, and so did the sun among the grapevine, and, above all, something like a dazzling bewilderment. Perhaps it was that swarm of lights—

green, gold and ruby among the cruel pieces of broken bottle glass, at the edge of the wall.)

It could hardly have been 3:15, in full sunlight, and we were surrounded by the burnt leaves. A green ashiness covered the dragon, like a rainfall of years. Manuel's face was thin and hard. And the deep hollows of his eyes, and the luster of his face, like faded wood, seemed on fire under the sun. His eyes were profoundly black with bluish corneas. I never saw eyes like his, eyes that made me forget—and I have forgotten, true enough—the rest of his features. And something strange that never happened with Borja, nor Guiem, nor Juan Antonio (who always found fault with me and tried to humiliate me) happened to me while looking at this boy (whom no one esteemed in the village; the son of a man dead because of his sinful ideas): I suddenly felt ridiculous, insignificant. And a wave of blood rushed to my face, and the echo of my blustering bravura, the aroma of my *Murattis,* my airs of superiority, and even my mint candies, came flashing across my memory like something idiotic and senseless. I did not know what more to say. I only stood there and looked at him and suddenly I realized, with one hand awkwardly extended toward him, how absurd my presence was: I, the granddaughter of old Práxedes, Borja's cousin, with Our Lady of the Angels part of my past. I thought: "He isn't furious." There was only a dark sadness in him, not for himself entirely, but rather, perhaps, for me too; as if he included me and joined me to him, squeezing me (as I squeezed in my hand a round, cold glass ball inside which snow fell). Into that sadness everything fit: my badly tied braids, which came apart at the ends and grazed the nape of my neck; my blouse, sloppily tucked into my skirt; my sandals with the straps still undone because of my hurried departure; and the sweat in which I was bathed.

"It seems awful," I said. And I noticed that my lips trembled and I was saying something I had not thought about until that moment, something still confused. "It seems an awful thing to do to you."

And in the midst of a strange shame, as if a way were opened in me for the expiation of confused, far-off faults which I did not understand but which licked my heels (faults committed perhaps against everything that surrounded me, including the Chink, Antonia, even perhaps Guiem himself; faults and sentiments I did not wish to recognize, like the fear or love of God), in the midst of all this, it seemed to me that a thin crust was cracking, with everything they forced me to stifle: Borja with his mockery; grandmother with her rigid customs, her laziness and indifference to us; and Aunt Emilia with her sticky uselessness. Suddenly, I stood up among all that. It was only I. "And why, why?" I said to myself. During that siesta of the earth, at that moment in which a dead dog infected the water of a well, it was I, only I, without understanding how, who was strangely (only possible at the defenseless age of fourteen) bewildered. And I added:

"It seems awful what they have done to you, what they're doing in this village, and all of them that live in it, they're all cowards and disgusting . . . So disgusting you could vomit. I hate them. I hate everyone here, everyone on this entire island, except for you!"

Hardly were they said when my words surprised me, and I was aware that my face was on fire. My skin was burning so that it felt as if the sun had been put inside me. And still I said to myself confusedly: "Well, I haven't drunk wine. There wasn't even a drop of brandy in Aunt Emilia's glass." He went on looking at me, only looking: without surprise, without hatred, or mockery, or affection. As if everything he saw and heard would be explained at the end of many years by other people who were not us. His hair shone coppery, burned by the sun and air. A very fine dust powdered his ankles and feet, which were shod in friar's sandals. His face was dust-covered, too. I continued:

"I don't know what I would give to get away from here! . . . Do you want me to help you carry the water?"

It was by his silence that I realized the harshness of my voice and how the echo of my words was trapped, like a hailstorm.

He said:

"No, no . . ."

Upon speaking, he seemed to wake up from something—perhaps, like me, from some dream—and he lowered his eyes. We remained facing one another, with the large jug between us, as if embarrassed. I was made desolate by my fourteen years and all that I had just told that boy who had asked us for the boat so that he might carry back the body of his father (assassinated

by the friends, or at least the supporters, of my grandmother). There was so much confusion in me, my ideas
were so muddled that I felt a great weight upon me.
I recall the buzzing of a bee, a thousand crackling sounds
among the leaves there to one side, in among the twigs
and branches of the orchard. I turned halfway around,
ridiculously dragging my feet so that my sandals would
not fall off.

I was going to leave, to leave there, when he finally
called me:

"No, it's not that!" he said. "Don't go off like that . . ."

He was watching me with a look which was so tired
that I thought: "He's also older than I, older than all
of us: but in a different way from Guiem." (In spite
of everything, the Chink had said he could not have
been more than sixteen.) I knew that Manuel had studied
with the friars, and there was something monastic about
him, perhaps in his voice, or in his eyes.

We lifted our heads. A dove, one of those grandmother
raised, swept over the Descent. Its flight seemed to graze
the roof of air. Its shadow crossed the ground, and something trembled in it: like a blue, falling star.

"If grandmother could see me! I often escape at this
hour . . . especially if Borja goes to the Naranjal.
They're pigs, they don't want to take me with them!"

Furious, I told him all about the Naranjal; and it was
as if a current of cold water gushed out (or just like
when Mauricia opened an infection in a finger for me
with her little knife, and I grew calm and feverless).
I was telling him everything, buckling my sandals, push-

ing my blouse back in my skirt. And he just stood there quietly, in silence. When I was finally silent, it seemed to me that he did not dare pick up the water jug and go away, nor stay either. Seeing his indecision, I again became saddened. "He doesn't want to be my friend," I said to myself. "He's afraid of grandmother. He thinks she wouldn't allow it. Though, perhaps . . ." But I was scared myself to think about it: I only wanted to let myself be carried along by that sweet river which seemed fatefully to propel me.

"Don't lose any more time. I'll keep you company."

I went to pick up the jug, but he was there before me. Without another word, he left the orchard. I went behind, and it seemed to me that he did not dare turn his head to see if I were following him. While he went down the Descent, I contemplated his back. He wore a white shirt, stained with earth, and blue pants. His bare ankles and sandaled feet were chestnut-colored, dulled by the fine dust which covered them.

His house stood at the foot of the Descent, very close to the sea. They had a few olive trees, somewhat off to one side, and toward the right a half-dozen almond trees. The orchard door, burned by the salt and the wind, was always open (just the opposite of our house, where everything was obstinately locked, as if hidden, as if jealously keeping to the shade). On the other hand, in Manuel's house the sun came in through all the holes, in an unexpected, almost anxious way. Manuel Taronjí's house, orchard and trees had all once belonged to Jorge

of Son Major. They said that Malene and the master of
Son Major had lived, some time ago, as man and wife.
At least, Borja said so. It pained me, suddenly, to know
it; I felt a strange and senseless pain. The Taronjí prop-
erties jutted into my grandmother's Descent. It seems
to me that grandmother did not care for them either,
but at least she never mentioned them. Perhaps, she
did not hate them, but only scorned them. But she always scorned things like that: like the relationship between Malene and Jorge of Son Major. Now, José
Taronjí was dead, and his son, who had never worked
the earth, had the nape of his neck burned by the sun,
and was plunged into the endless fire of the earth, as
if soaked in something that was for me unattainable and
hermetic. I remember Borja's expression of angry fear
when Manuel took the *Leontina* from us and carried
it off. And I, why, if I did not really know him—didn't
I really know Manuel?—did I feel a necessity to tell him
so many things that neither Borja nor Juan Antonio
would have heard from me? To tell him, perhaps, only:
"I don't understand anything about the things that happen in life or in the world, or around me: from the
birds down to the earth, from the sky down to the water,
I don't understand a thing." The world with which they
all threatened me, from grandmother to the Chink, was
like a punishment. "Whether or not the world is atrocious, I don't know, but at least it's beyond my comprehension." And looking at Manuel's back, the nape of his
neck and fire-colored hair, I said to myself: "If he knew

about my doll Gorogó . . . would he be able to understand it?" He was a stranger, that boy, that poor boy, a Jew from the lowest class in the village, with a murdered father and a mother of dubious reputation. Why did it matter to me so much? "Why should these things be?"

Arriving at the orchard door, he turned to look at me. And then I realized how his enormous black eyes glistened, a fierce glistening which left me motionless, without the courage to cross the open doorway. And I told myself that he probably thought: "Stop there, you little hysteric, this is my kingdom, here I'm the master: go back to your house and your old woman, your selfish old grandmother, your hypocrites, your hidden scoundrels. Go back to your closed house with its moldy corners and its rats which run like distressed souls in hell and your gold-plate dishes, the gift of the king. Go on, go back: this house is my house and you'll never understand it, you stupid, ridiculous creature." I stood quietly and looked for Gorogó who was also very concerned, there under my blouse, over my pounding heart. "Foolish creature, go back to your cigarettes and your drinking parties for badly brought-up children, go back to your declensions and French translations, and to your lessons in graceful walking, under the bamboo cane. Go back, go on back, they'll marry you off to a soft, slimy man rotten with money, or with a bestial whip like Uncle Álvaro's." The doves flew overhead toward Son Major, and their shadows were like a rainfall of dark, fugitive drops, slanted along the earth, rushing beneath our feet like leaves pushed by the wind. I was afraid, as on that day, as on that morning under the fig tree, when the majestic cock of Son Major looked at me so ferociously.

At that moment Manuel said:

"Will you wait for me? . . ."

And when he disappeared behind the wall, I was still saying yes—truly, a little hysteric, a little idiot—shaking my head up and down, like Gorogó.

5

"At first I lived with them," I told him lying on the ground, under the almond trees. "At least, I remember something like that . . . but I was very small. They say that my grandmother would not have anything to do with my father. They lived together quite a while, but then, apparently, they were divorced . . ."

"How terrible," said Manuel in a low voice.

He, too, lay face down on the ground and we were very close to one another. We dared look at each other only once in a while. I spoke in a very low voice, and when I turned my face toward him, his eyes were very close to mine. I could feel my heart pounding against the earth, and it seemed to me I could almost hear his.

"Terrible, why? I don't remember anything . . . almost nothing . . . They sent me off to school, in Madrid in the Calle del Cisne; the school was called Saint Maur . . . When I went back home, they were never there. Never, neither he nor she. But it didn't matter to me! Besides, I had Gorogó."

And he—I would never have imagined it—had Gorogó in his hands. In his dark hands, with fresh calluses and scratches (he was not used to working the soil), he held my Negrito. He turned him between his fingers, looked at him, and probably did not understand him—what difference did it make? He listened to me seriously, quietly, with his big eyes shining in the shade of the trees. There below, behind us, the solemn breathing of the sea sounded. Behind us the green and ocher light mounted, rising over the land of the Descent. Between the bent shadows of the trees, the light slid over us, along the length of our bodies. It was like a long, thick dream, that never would repeat itself. We were bathed in a glowing green, and there above, the furious gold and red of the big sun seemed to spy on us. We knew that the sun could do nothing with us while we were like that, side by side, hardly daring to look at one another. Out of the corner of my eye (in the way grandmother disapproved) I could see his amber ear covered with soft fuzz; it was like a shell to which I felt like nearing my own ear in order to hear his sea. And because of that I told him so many things. In a low voice, as if it were only for me or Gorogó:

"And then, she died. But I was in school, and I almost don't remember . . . Mauricia, you know—my father's nanny—made my lunch, and told me many stories. She was very old. And when she died . . ."

And I said "she" and "he," and Manuel never, never asked me who "they" were. He never asked me anything, he never tried to draw me out: he only listened, at my side, silently. (Like a lost little animal, like myself.)

"When she died, he sent me to the country with Mauricia. But that was such a different kind of land!"

Manuel asked, also in a quiet voice, and without looking at me:

"Did you like it?"

"Yes. I liked it so much!" (And I became silent and it all came rushing back to me: the forests and the river, and a knot in my throat. And Andersen, and *Alice Through the Looking Glass,* and Gulliver . . . and *A Captain Who Was Fifteen,* and those miniature rivers, traced with a stick in the clay . . . The rivers that I made for the gnomes, in the damp earth of the ditches. And those yellow flowers, shaped like the sun, which I put inside the locks of doors, and the screams of the ravens, which imitated the echo, in the caves; and the voice of Mauricia: *"I am a small raven, a very tiny raven, without bread or salt . . ."*

"Matia, a package from Papa has arrived.")

"I had a cardboard theater," I told him.

He raised his head:

"Ah, I did too. *He* sent it to me . . ."

I turned to look at him. He was very pale, and he said in a rush:

"He sent me books too. I liked to read a lot. They were almost always travel books. He had traveled so much! He spent his life traveling around the islands in his boat."

His arm was raised, as if tracing an imaginary route in the air. I looked at him, and my blood rushed to my face and I had a mad desire to tell him: "No, don't tell me any more, don't tell me hidden things about men and women because I don't want to know anything about a world I don't understand. Let me alone, let me alone, I still can't make it out." But the same thing that happened to me happened to him: like the infection that Mauricia opened with the tiny knife. He was in profile, framed in a halo of green light from the almond trees. Like small animals against the stony earth, we slid downward along the Descent. Only at that moment did I realize we were sliding senselessly downward. There was something menacing, like a threat, at our backs. And he added:

"He sent me souvenirs from all those countries . . ."

And all at once, as if his breathing would give out:

"And he wanted . . . he said, for me to be like him, perhaps. But he frightened me, and at times I thought I'd stay in the monastery, with the monks, forever."

Then he raised his hand and it fell on mine. He pressed my hand against the ground, as if he wanted to hold me back, so I might not fall downward, into the great threat. Into the thick, blue, hallucinating vertigo that I could sense from the tiny plaza where they burned Jews, over the cliff. As if with him, with his hand, with my childhood which went astray, with our ignorance and goodness, I might want to sink our hands forever, to nail them in the still pure, old, wise earth.

"Oh, yes?" I said, with a thread of a voice, that only could be heard very close to me. And maybe he did not hear it, because he went on saying:

"I was his favorite among all the others. At first I didn't realize it. I lived with the monks. The abbot was a cousin of his and he was kind to me. I came to the island only during Christmas vacations . . ."

He remained thoughtful and added:

"But the last time I came she had a talk with me, and I realized the whole truth. I'm somewhat different from the rest, not so clever . . . Even up there I was too innocent. And she said to me: *'Son, you're too good, you're already fifteen.'* And still, when she spoke to me, it seemed I was older than all of them."

He covered his face with his hands and I put mine on the nape of his neck, which was soft and warm. He did not move until I took it away, and then he turned to look at me:

"That day, I renounced all the privileges I received from him. I realized that my place was with them, there, in that house: with José and Malene, with my sister and brother, María and Tomeu . . . and above all with him, with Taronjí," he said the last name very quickly as if he were breathing it. "I had to be at his side! Because he was gnawed by hatred and I had to be at his side, when everyone looked at him with mockery, or as an enemy. I thought: 'Manuel, this is your house, your family.' Because, one doesn't pick out a family, it's given to you!"

Something tightened in my chest. (Oh, my poor black Gorogó, the False Chimney Sweep.) He continued:

"I understood that my brother and sister lived a different kind of life from mine, and that no one wanted to help them . . . and as for her, no woman would speak to her when she went to the village. And I heard her tell things to José Taronjí . . . she was so bitter! Because he loved her and suffered because of everything that had happened before and what was still happening. I almost believed he hated me too. And then I thought: *I have to get him to love me.* And I also had to love him some day."

I was afraid, fearful of hearing those things. It was something so new for me! Not the discovery of the secret of Manuel's life—a dirty secret of men and women for which he was not to blame—but rather the way I came to learn about the strange world: the frightful, dreadful world with which they threatened Borja and me, from which the Chink fled desperately. The world which Guiem and Mariné maliciously referred to, the world which, apparently, belonged to people like Jorge of Son Major. In spite of myself, I did not understand him:

"And . . . you stayed with them?"

"Yes, I've stayed with them."

Grandmother's doves returned: at that moment they perched among the almond trees. They were like greenish-blue shadows over our heads. They made strange crackling sounds. Something vibrated in the air like drops of very fine glass.

"Now you're on the outside too. I mean, outside the barrier. You understand, do you? From the Taronjí, the delegate, and all the rest. And, probably, from my grandmother too . . ."

"I know it," he said.

"Aren't you afraid?"

He waited before answering:

"Yes, at times I am. It's not exactly fear I feel, but something like a great sorrow."

When he said *sorrow,* a suffocating, slow weight seemed really to roll along the Descent. He picked up an almond: it was hollow and he let it fall. It showed us its hole, black and rotten like a bad mouth. If I had not been fourteen, perhaps I would have wanted to cry. At that moment, I felt his sorrow as if it were mine, something like an embarrassing repentance: "Because of that, this boy is not with Guiem or Borja. Because of that, he is not with any of us." Or perhaps, he was with all of us. "Because he is so good . . ." But was he really good? Was I bad? Were Borja or the Chink bad? What confusion! And Jorge of Son Major, behind his walls, was hiding the horror of his own old age by cultivating flowers.

"Manuel," I said. "You're too . . ."

I did not know what to call him. I felt almost irritated at the sight and sound of him. But I wanted him to be part of our world: of our treasures, the *Young Simón,* Mariné's café . . . even to the point of letting him go to the Naranjal with the other boys. But what did he have to do with all that? What did he have to do with anyone in the world? I looked at his hands, which were unused to work, his scratched fingers. And he said:

"No, don't you believe it . . . My place was here, among the bitter ones, among all this misery . . . When the trouble came, I had already decided to stay. But, you already know: they've killed him."

A tiny green lizard came out from under a stone. The two of us remained very quiet looking at it. Our eyes were close to the ground and, from between the grasses, the lizard looked at us. His tiny eyes, like pinheads, were sharp and terrible. For moments it seemed like the awful dragon of Saint George, in the stained-glass window of Santa María. I said to myself: "He belongs among the men: the ugly things of men and women." And I was at the point of growing and changing into a woman. Or probably I already was. My hands felt cold, in the midst of the heat. "No, no, let them wait a little longer . . . a little longer." But who had to wait? It was I, only I, who was a traitor to myself at every turn. It was I, I myself, and no one else, who was betraying Gorogó and the Is-land of Never-Never. I thought: "What kind of monster am I now?" I closed my eyes in order not to feel the tiny-but-enormous look of the dragon of Saint George. "What kind of monster am I that I no longer have my child-hood, and am still far from being, in any way, a woman?"

I wanted to get away from so much grief, and I said:

"And the man from Son Major, doesn't he call you sometimes? Doesn't he want to know anything about you any more? He'll think you've betrayed him."

"Yes, he has called me twice. You know the man with the guitar: the one who has lived with him for a long time. He used to take him around before in the *Delfín*. Now he is very old, but he still sings songs he likes a lot . . . Sanamo is his name and he puts red roses behind his ear. He says he's his only true friend. Well, Sanamo came to the orchard, behind the olive trees, when I was gathering the almonds with my brother, sister and mother. And he called me."

(I imagined him like the devil in Paradise, behind the trees, with a dark rose at his temple.)

"I answered him: 'I can't, tell him I can't. I have to help my mother and family. I would certainly like to go. Tell him that I appreciate it. And also tell him that I love him a great deal, but while these people live I can't return to him.'"

And when he said *"I love him a great deal"* his voice quavered, so warm and close to me, that a furious envy seized me.

I had a fleeting desire to be bad, cruel. (And I could think of nothing to say against the words that pained me: *"I love him a great deal."* Only foolish things occurred to me like: "Well, I love Gorogó a great deal: well, I love that crystal ball a great deal, and I love a great deal, and a great deal . . ." What an enormous ache filled me! How is it possible to feel so much pain at fourteen? And it was an endless pain.)

I stood up brusquely, pressing my palms on the ground, while the tiny-toothed stones stuck to my hands. The lizard fled, terrified; Manuel looked at me from below, his mouth half-open, as if surprised. As if someone might have ripped the veil which we had hidden ourselves behind. And I said:

"Let's go! Let's go there."

"Where?"

"To Son Major."

"No. What are you saying?"

He got up. As we had never been so close to each other, it was only now I saw that he was taller than I. I thought:

"I wish he'd think I was older than he: at least eighteen."

"Come on with me, silly."

And I knew—at that moment I knew it for the first time—that he would go wherever I asked.

I began to walk, very sure of myself. And even if I could not hear him, I knew that he was following me, that he would always follow me. (And how much it hurt later. Or, at least, how much it pained me for some time, which now already seems lost.)

THE *BONFIRES*

TOWARD the middle of September the grapes ripened. The mayor's wife sent grandmother the first bunches on a glazed earthenware tray decorated with blue and yellow flowers. An embroidered linen cloth covered them. Grandmother took one between two fingers. It was as fresh and beautiful as her diamond was ugly and dirty. She tried it and spit the skin into her hand.

"They're sour," she commented. "I figured as much."

The grapes, like pearled drops, remained forgotten on the tray.

Borja, who had been looking at me nastily all day, turned toward grandmother and observed:

"The ones from Son Major will be sweet."

Those words were meant for me. He delicately washed the tips of his fingers and wiped them with his napkin. He looked like a little Pontius Pilate.

"Serve the coffee, Antonia," grandmother said.

She never would answer when Son Major was mentioned. (I once asked the Chink: "Why is grandmother mad at Saint George?" "Don't be irreverent, Miss Matia," he answered. But, as he understood perfectly, he added: "Why do lords and peasants stay at odds?" And he crudely rubbed his index finger against his thumb.)

"Grandmother, may we go now?" Borja asked. "We'd like to walk for a while along the Descent, before class . . ."

Grandmother scrutinized me, and in spite of myself, I blushed. "Borja has something to tell me."

"You'd do well to prepare yourself," said grandmother. "Monsignor Mayol is looking for a new school for you. And after the trouble you caused us at Our Lady of the Angels, I hope you'll reflect before you do something you shouldn't."

Then she looked at my cousin:

"You're also going to begin your schooling again, Borja. This situation is lasting longer than we thought it would, and we are looking for a proper school for you."

She paused and added:

"The war ought not interrupt our daily life any further. War is a horrible thing."

"War?" I said to myself. "What war? This rotten silence, this detestable deathly silence."

"I hate war," grandmother went on. "We ought to go on living and ignoring it as much as possible."

"When will we be going to school?" Borja asked, with a smile which seemed to anticipate from such fatal news the sweetest of honeys, or the fulfillment of something very much desired.

"After Christmas," grandmother said, putting her hand out for her pills. "It won't be possible before that. You both need sound preparation so as not to expose me to a new failure."

She looked significantly at the Chink, who bent his head. It was almost a way of dismissing him. What would the Chink do in that house when we would no longer need him? It seemed to me that when Antonia served the coffee her fingers trembled.

We kissed grandmother's hand and Aunt Emilia's cheek and went out. We each ran to our own room to take off our uncomfortable clothes; when we came out again, we looked messy, but felt very comfortable.

Borja was already waiting for me on the Descent, seated under an almond tree, opening and closing Guiem's knife. His hair fell over his forehead.

"Hypocrite, little lowlife," he said.

I smiled, feigning pride before his insults, and I began walking down the path to the pier, where we kept the *Leontina*. He was following behind. I heard him jump the retaining wall, like a buck.

"Traitor, ignoramus," he went on.

He was really angry and spiteful. When we got to the pier, we stopped. We were out of breath and panting.

"We're throwing you out of the gang. Out! Out with traitors!"

I shrugged my shoulders, although my knees were shaking.

"I don't want to be part of your gang," I said. "I have my own friends."

"I know all about it. Some friends you've got! Grand-mother will find out."

"It won't be because you tell her, I don't suppose."

"No, of course not: it won't be because of me."

"Well, then . . ."

I was beginning to understand my cousin. All I had to do was feign indifference in the face of his bravado to exasperate him. Was it perhaps for that reason that he hated Manuel, who never showed the slightest interest, either for or against? Was it perhaps because of that same reason he secretly, passionately adored Jorge of Son Major?

He seized me so violently by the wrist I thought he was going to break it.

"Come here, senseless," he said. And he softened his voice, as he did when we met on the loggia at night.

(It suddenly seemed as if a long time had passed since those conversations, since those furtive cigarettes.)

"I'm telling you this for your own good, you big double fool. Don't you know who he is? Don't you know that nobody speaks to them? His mother . . . well, and his father, how did he end up?"

It was the middle of September and the earth was damp, the leaves, golden brown, piled up on the ground of the Descent. It was the siesta hour, like that other time (but how different). I said:

"José Taronjí wasn't his father . . . How naive of you!"

I began to laugh and walk along the edge of the cliff.

I looked over my shoulder, and I saw him following me. I heard his agitated breathing.

"What are you saying? You're bad! . . ."

I turned around. I felt wildly happy then.

"It can't be," he said. He was breaking down, fearing a name I had not pronounced. "It isn't true . . . that's only gossip. He's a Taronjí, a dirty Jew, a son of a . . ."

He never used words like that. He blushed and I felt sorry for him. (It was the worst thing I could have said to him: "Manuel is not a son of José Taronjí.") Borja sat down on a rock, as if his legs suddenly could not support him, or as if he did not want me to see his quivering. His lips were drained of color, and he repeated:

"It can't be."

We could hear the sea at our feet. Between the trees, and toward the left, Malene and Manuel's house shone brilliant white.

"And . . . is it true that you go *there?*" he asked.

I nodded my head cruelly in order to take pleasure in his sorrow. (And it was not true, we had not gone *there,* as he imagined. I never had enough courage. I was irritated with myself because of my cowardliness. The first time, on that afternoon, when I said to Manuel, "Come on with me," he followed me in spite of himself, against his will. We climbed along the road over the cliff. At the outskirts of the village, almost at the beginning of the forest, lay Son Major, its high walls glittering in the afternoon sun, and the palms, dirty green and disheveled, shooting up beyond the walls. The closer we came, the more afraid I grew, since Manuel had told me the truth. Through the green iron gate, Manuel and I, very close together, looked at the red flowers, which reminded me of the almost black rose that Sanamo wore over his ear. Once we heard his guitar. Manuel and I, silent as thieves, were pressed against the white wall of Son Major, one in front of the other, like two wandering shadows or two stray dogs. Sanamo's music floated across the walls, and hearing it we held our breath. The murmur of music rending the warm air. There was no human voice: only the music of the strings, the sun and wind on the corner. One afternoon, well into September, Manuel and I were leaning up against the wall, looking at each other like strangers, and I recalled those words he once had said: *"Tell him I love him a great deal."*

The wind screamed above the cliff, and Manuel said to me: "I always heard that wild savage wind when I went to Son Major at Christmas." I thought of the Chink, who had said: "That man, good God: wild and savage," on one occasion when Borja had commented, "They all say I look like Jorge of Son Major." And even if Borja would say to Guiem and his friends, in order to frighten them: "My father can have as many men shot as he wants to," or "He has had more men hung from trees than there are grapes in a bunch"—even if he might say all this, he did not want to look like Uncle Álvaro. He wanted to look like Jorge of Son Major, of the *Delfín* and the Greek islands. "That man, that wind, wild and savage.")

"So you both went to Son Major . . . so it's not just an invention of Guiem's."

I went on nodding, although I began to weaken inside. "And him . . . did you see him?"

I did not answer. I was losing courage because of so much lying. I felt pity for Borja, even though I did not understand what fascinated him so much, why everyone was fascinated by that man, though almost no one ever saw him.

Borja smiled, raising his lip in the way which showed his fierce eyeteeth. And said:

"Get out of here! Leave me alone! You big liar . . . I don't want to see you again."

Then the Chink's voice called to us between the trees. ("Latin, hateful Latin.") And I said, in order to make matters worse:

"Manuel could get the better of you in Latin. He knows more Latin than Monsignor Mayol. Next to him, you and I are mere nothings."

We went back home in silence. The Chink was waiting for us quietly, his hands crossed over his stomach and his eyes hidden behind the green lenses.

At twilight Juan Antonio and the administrator's boys arrived, whistling among the cherry trees in the garden.

"Borja, Guiem's gang is starting trouble!"

These were not days of truce. The sky seemed to be covered by a big, swollen, reddish cloud. Borja jumped from the hammock, and glared at me.

"Who are you with?" he demanded.

"With you."

He shrugged his shoulders, but he was smiling. He

threw his book, which he was no longer reading, on the floor, and said:

"It's not a thing for you anyway."

The Chink approached nervously.

"Come on with me, Chinky, come on with me, pal," my cousin said.

He was ecstatic and he laughed to one side, as only he knew how to do. The Chink blushed.

Juan Antonio and the administrator's boys waited at the iron gate. Juan Antonio was sweating:

"They're in the plaza! They've started bonfires and they're waving butcher hooks at us . . . let's go and teach them a lesson!"

"And your friend?" Borja asked me in a whisper, close to my ear. "Whose side is he on, theirs or ours?"

The Chink looked at us. The green of his glasses left shadows on his cheeks. He said:

"Miss Matia, stay here, I beg you . . . stay here."

"I'm going," I answered, just to be contrary and not out of any real desire to go along. "I always go with Borja."

"Let's go, Chink, Mr. Preceptor, my beloved!" Borja guffawed strangely.

The Chink broke off a cherry branch and his hands trembled:

"I can't, really, Borja . . . I can't . . . your grandmother . . ."

"To hell with the old dame! Come on, old boy. You haven't got much time left with us: you already heard, they're going to kick you out after Christmas."

It seemed too cruel to me, but then Borja was deeply

hurt, tormented by what I had revealed to him; he did not know what he was saying. The Chink made no answer, but the vein on his forehead swelled like a river about to overflow. For the first time it occurred to me that his hatred might also be dangerous and overwhelming. And that it would finally burst one day. I offered him my hand:

"Come on with me," I said with a mocking grimace. "Come on with me, sir."

Lauro the Chink broke the cherry branch between his fingers, and I heard its crackling sound. Borja, Juan Antonio, and the administrator's boys began to run madly toward the village. Slowly, the Chink and I followed them.

"One of these days he'll get into real trouble," the Chink said. "One of these days something will happen to him that we won't be able to keep from his grandmother or his mother . . . Miss Matia, if only you had some influence over him . . . the crazy kid!"

His voice quavered, perhaps out of anger. But it was still restrained, with the treacherous sweetness of the meek.

2

"*It was something to see how their flesh caught fire, how the flames licked their entrails: how their stomachs were ripped in two, from top to bottom, with a demoniacal brilliance, and . . . ,*" said the book which Borja found in grandfather's bedroom. It explained how they burned

Jews alive. It was the same plaza where those scenes had occurred centuries before.

The first stars of early evening shone and the heat of the day gave way to a humid dankness which came down from the woods. At that hour the ruins turned sinister, and it was true that the flagstones at the center of the plaza seemed blackened, and the earth burnt. Even the moss, which covered it all, seemed invaded with the cruel mildew of a cemetery or a well.

They had lit the bonfires. The biggest one in the middle; another, toward the cliff; the third, at the entrance of the woods. The black, fierce oaks rose somberly along the hillside, and they had the familiar odor of those of my country.

The rusty iron hooks were usually buried in secret places. They had three: one belonging to Guiem (bigger and blacker than the others, which probably was used to hang large carcasses), another belonging to Toni of Abrés, and the third one belonging to the cripple (no one understood how he had gotten his hands on it, but in any case he would not give it up for anything in the world). When Guiem's gang unearthed the butcher hooks, it meant war. They would taunt Borja, Juan Antonio, the administrator's children, the Chink and me, from morning to night. They lit bonfires in the plaza of the Jews, and if we would not pay any attention to them they burned straw dolls, which signified their triumph over Borja and Juan Antonio.

They stole the hooks from the butcher shop, heroically and conscientiously: first one, then another, and another.

Jaime, the butcher, swore he would kill the person who stole another one. Borja and Juan Antonio dreamed of someday finding the secret places where they were buried. To me, they suggested something brutal, perhaps because they brought back the memory of the head hung at the door of the butcher shop. The eye, with its swollen blue pupil between rivulets of blood, staring intently out to one side, full of dumb hate, seemed the symbol of the wrath between Borja and Guiem. Even today I cannot pass in front of a butcher shop without feeling a crawling sensation of disgust and fear down my spine.

In the early evening shadows the bonfires blazed vigorously. Some village boys stood around and threw dry branches brought from the forest into the fire. When they saw Borja and Juan Antonio, followed by the administrator's sons, they started to run and then stopped at a spot some distance away, lined up in a row to witness the encounter. In the blue light, the bonfires transformed everything into night.

Smudged and dark, Guiem came out of the woods. He pulled down his sweater sleeve until it covered his fingers, so that the hook stuck out, twisted and weird. (*Captain Hook fought Peter Pan along the cliffs of the Island of Never-Never*. Borja, an exiled Peter Pan, like me, *the boy who did not want to grow up returned home at night and found the window closed*. Borja never seemed as wispy as at that moment. *He did spring cleaning at the time of the gathering of the leaves, in the forest of Lost Children*. And the same Lost Children were all too grown up, suddenly, for playing; and too childlike, sud-

denly, to start life, in a world that we did not want—
didn't we want it?—to know.)

"Judas, Judas, Judas!"

The Chink stopped at the entrance to the plaza, his
hands crossed, sunk into silence. I saw his trembling profile, his scant, thin mustache concealing the corners of
his mouth. And suddenly he seemed so young! Until that
moment I had never realized he was a boy, only a boy;
hardly older than us, filled to the brim with the dirty
things of men and women; sunk up to his shoulders in
the world, in that bottomless well into which all of us
were already slipping.

"Judas, Judas!"

The name floated toward us carried on the wind that
swirled the long locks of flame on the bonfires. A red
glow vibrated, like the surface of stirred water, over the
chipped flagstones of the plaza, the cracked columns
where a portico was ranged in former days, and the decaying huts with their useless doors securely locked. And
rats and weasels, bats, lizards, and patent-leather cock-
roaches would run terrified through crevices and broken
staircases. The locks were dark eyes that peered inward,
only inward, and they were pierced by threads of red
light; now they served to rouse tiny cold-blooded lizards,
like the one on the Descent that stared at me so fixedly.
Terrified by the odor of fire and the screams of the boys
they would scurry away.

The Chink shivered, perhaps caught in his secret, which
suddenly I did not want to know anything about. It was
as if that breakneck race toward the bottomless well of

life, which I had undertaken since my expulsion from Our Lady of the Angels, were spied on by insects, rats, and lizards, by moist and pinkish earthworms; and I wanted to scream and say: "Oh no, no, stop me, please. Stop me, I didn't know where I was running, I don't want to know anything more." (But I had already jumped over the wall and left Kay and Gerda in their garden on the rooftop.) And looking at the Chink, at my side, I felt my first grown-up pity; I wanted to give him my hand and tell him: "Don't pay any attention, they're only ignorant children. Forgive them; they don't know what they're doing." And at one and the same time I was ashamed of that first adult sentiment and I was frightened and pained at myself, my words, my pity.

"Who's going into the forest? Who would like to take a walk through the woods?"

Guiem was triumphant. I think they had drunk wine. All of them—Guiem, Ramón, Toni of Abrés, and the cripple—had stained lips and their shirts hung out of their pants. They were sweating, their round heads poking up, shining in the night. Borja was alone, standing (*goodbye, Peter Pan, goodbye, I'll no longer be able to go with you on the next Spring Cleaning: you'll have to sweep all the fallen leaves alone*), still and golden in the middle of the plaza, and in his eyes there was something reminiscent of Uncle Álvaro ("He shoots whom he wants, he is a general and drinks to the king"). He was smiling with his lip turned up, contracted over his small cannibal eyeteeth (Doña Práxedes, fiercely indifferent, tasting sour grapes, dismissing useless preceptors). At his side were his miserable bodyguards, brutal and cowardly, Juan Antonio (trapped by the devil) and the administrator's boys (unwillingly dragged along by Doña Práxedes' hateful grandson: pious because of Doña Práxedes, studying in summer like Doña Práxedes' grandchildren). At the entrance of the little plaza, as if protecting the world which was escaping us, minute by minute, the Chink trembled.

Borja went directly into the woods. Lauro began to run after him, scared:

"Careful, Borja! Borja, don't take the carbine with you! Borja, you're crazy! They'll kill you . . . something will happen, and grandmother . . . !"

He had forgotten the formal address, the "Your lady grandmother," he had forgotten everything, absolutely everything.

I stood motionless, waiting. Juan Antonio, the big coward, edged in among the trees, little by little. The cripple, brandishing his hook, was watching him.

"It's nothing," he said. "It's nothing."

They all went off. Only the last low crackling of the bonfire remained in the small plaza. Borja carried the scorched straw doll in his hand, the doll they had dressed in a sloppy sweater so that it would look like him. I do not know how, but that shapeless and half-burnt object, rescued at the last moment by Borja, looked like him. Yes, it looked like him. He waved it high, in his right hand. His left arm was contracted, and blood trickled down through his sleeve. He had beautiful blood, so red it seemed orange.

"It's nothing," he repeated. "I gave him a good one! That'll teach them! They're always throwing the business about the carbine in my face, well, today I went in with my hands in my pockets . . ."

He was pale, but he smiled. I never saw him with such shining eyes, so handsome. Guiem had caught him on the forearm with the hook. The Chink wrapped up his injured arm with his handkerchief. It was not anything serious, but drops of sweat were rolling down the Chink's forehead. Once more we could feel ourselves surrounded by an impenetrable silence. The shouts of the previous hours were as remote as a dream.

"We went in . . . ," he wanted to explain in detail, "and right at the beginning, in those trees over there, I told him: 'I haven't got the carbine.' And he answered: 'That's good.' But he didn't throw away his hook, and we hid. I saw his hair shining among the leaves. I could follow him because of that . . . until he leaped out at me, suddenly. Well, he weighs a lot, but he's clumsy. My father showed me how to fight. You know about that, don't you, Chink? . . . You know very well that I . . ."

"Yes," replied the Chink.

And it seemed to me he was deeply and mysteriously forlorn.

"It didn't last long," said Carlos, the youngest son of the administrator. "You won right away!"

"But they have their honor," Juan Antonio observed. "You have to say that for them. They went off without looking for more . . ."

"But they only had it in for me," Borja answered. And he looked at me: "Because of that Jew, they say. They know he's a friend of Matia."

I looked at the ground. The Chink raised his head:

"Good God, Miss Matia!"

Borja got up:

"They think Manuel is going to become part of our gang, because Matia . . . All right, that's over. Isn't that true, Matia, that it's over?"

I turned my eyes away, and became silent.

We returned home. The Chink kept saying:

"Heavens, come to my room, my mother will take care of your arm. That way, your lady grandmother won't find out anything . . ."

We still had an hour before supper. We entered through the door on the Descent and went silently up to the Chink's room.

He lit the lamp on the small table. There were the flowers as usual, the reproductions nailed onto the dormer ceiling, so they could be seen from the bed. The speckled mirror, his books, his ceramic jars, the clay figures, and the *ciurells,* the painted clay-figure whistles from Ibiza, filled his room. When he lit the lamp, his large yellow hands were illuminated so they looked like an enormous butterfly. He said:

"Wait . . . I'll call my mother."

The window was still open and a piece of fresh, humid

sky confronted us. We could see a star. Borja came close to kiss me:

"Matia, Matia, I beg you . . ."

I thought he was going to cry and for the first time he seemed more of a child than I; even though he had bridged the gap in years to manhood, his bravado was dissipated, and he was undone. (As I was that afternoon, next to Manuel.) He said:

"Matia, tell me it isn't true, tell me."

"But it is true, Borja! It's not my fault. He is Jorge's own son. He really is. . . ."

He bit his lips. (Those lips that always seemed too red for a boy.) He squeezed his left forearm with his right hand, which surely did not hurt him as much as that revelation.

"It can't be . . . That fellow! Matia, you know Jorge is a relative of ours. He's mad at grandmother, I know that. But that's all foolishness. He's of our blood . . ."

"But why is it so important to you?" I said, no longer able to contain myself. "I'm sorry it hurts you to know, but it's the absolute truth. And besides, everybody knows it. He loved Malene, and Manuel is their child. Then he married Malene off to his administrator, to keep up appearances. Everybody knows it. And he made a gift of that land there, in grandmother's way . . . I can't help it, Borja, life's like that."

And when I said that I felt stupid and smug. (What idiocy! I had heard maids say "life's like that.")

Borja recovered his pride. He raised his head and looked at me almost with hatred:

"You little idiot!"—he mimicked my voice—" 'Life's like that!' You little idiot."

The door creaked and Antonia came in. She seemed a little more pale than usual, almost green. The shadows of her nose and eyes, on her dry, long face, were accentuated in the lamplight, making it look like a mask. She carried cotton, iodine, and a washbasin with water. Over her arm she carried a fringed towel.

"Master Borja! . . . San Bruno help us! . . ."

The parakeet, perched on Antonia's head, looked at us with his round, irritated eyes. His long dark tail, slanted toward the woman's forehead, seemed like a restless, throbbing flower.

"Let's see that arm . . . My goodness, good God . . ."

And she allowed a concealed sigh to escape; it was too sincere to have anything to do with Borja's wound. "She probably cries in her room sometimes," I said to myself. Framed in the doorway, the Chink stood still, with his green glasses.

"Like this, hold it like this, tight . . ."

Borja tightened the cotton against the wound. I sat down on the edge of the bed, swinging my legs. Borja began to whistle softly. He was nervous and his breathing was irregular.

Antonia turned toward the Chink. Her voice filled the room, as she said hoarsely:

"Come in, son . . ."

Borja and I looked at the Chink. "Come in, son." We had never heard Antonia pronounce that word; she never called him in that way. "We knew that he was her son, that was all," I thought. "But we never felt it." Suddenly, the small room was invaded with something like a beating of wings. The woman looked at that boy—he was a poor boy, an ugly boy, too big for his legs—standing in the doorway. The Chink came in and sat down, his shoulders bent over, in a chair. His forehead was moist, and that woman's hand—it was not Antonia, oh no, it seemed like Mauricia's hand, or perhaps some other hand I had known, or lost, or only wanted—that wide hand relaxed its usual stiffness and pushed back the boy's hair. He raised his head, took off his glasses, and looked at her. And for the first time—with what pain, or remorse, or whatever it might have been: perhaps only grief—I saw his eyes. They looked at one another, her glance penetrating his. And I remembered, absurdly, a phrase that my friend had once said: "My place is here." (In the world, that is, of men and women. And something moved within my breast, something that foundered like a walnut shell at sea.) "That's enough!" Borja said, in a faraway voice. (In a world of naughty, capricious boys, with their infantile stubbornness, stupid grudges, and excessive admiration for Beings like the wind, who burned their *Delfín* on a distant Greek beach.)

"That's good enough! Thank you, Antonia. Thanks, Lauro."

They had taken away the photograph which was stuck in the corner of the mirror. Perhaps they kept it in a book, or in some dog-eared portfolio, or in some pocket, over the heart.

Tiny Gondoliero flew about with a dull beating of wings, and Borja began to laugh.

I was already in bed, without Gorogó, my right hand under the pillow which was still cool. Night entered in bands through the slats of the shutters. And I heard: *tac, tac, tac*. "No, Borja, please," I said to myself. For a long time we had not gone to the loggia, our hidden refuge, to smoke cigarettes and whisper to each other. "Oh no, Borja, all that's over." But the tapping continued. I threw my sweater over my shoulders and went into the little hall. The window gave onto the loggia, and I jumped through.

I made him out at the other end, all huddled up. The red eye of a cigarette shone in the darkness, like a one-eyed animal. A tiny column of smoke rose toward the arches. I crossed the loggia, crouching, and joined him. He was seated, his legs crossed, propped against the wall.

"Come here, closer," he said, in a low voice.

Behind the arches spread a pale blue sky, with widely spaced stars. I sat down at his side, and he put his arm around my shoulder.

"Matia, you think you know a lot, don't you?"

As I did not say anything, he went on:

"You don't know anything about anything . . . !"

I looked at him out of the corner of my eye. I saw his eyes shining in the light of the moon. His cheek grazed mine.

"I'm going to confess something to you," he said.

He was talking in that whispering tone which we always used on the loggia, and in spite of myself, I felt attracted again to him and his world.

"I'm going to open your eyes: you're an innocent child. But since you think you know so much . . . Well, I'll tell you something. You know, the Chink . . ."

I was afraid again. Afraid, almost dizzy with fear.

"Keep quiet!" I said.

I tried to get away from him, but he held me firmly.

"The Chink," he continued, "does everything I order him to do, because, if I wanted to, I could tell other things about him to grandmother."

In spite of myself, I asked:

"What things?"

And I remembered the one time I went to the Naranjal, the day in which the Chink, Borja and I went on an excursion, and returned in the afternoon. Borja went on talking in the darkness of the loggia, but I almost did not listen to what he began to tell me, because all at once as in a dream, that day was coming back to me. A very distinct dream, raw and real, with a revealing meaning. I felt a terror which made my hands damp and chilled my whole being. It was the month of March. The war had not yet broken out, and they had just expelled me from Our Lady of the Angels. A golden mist dimmed my eyes, numbing them.

(I remember: "When the new stars come out we won't be here any longer," said the Chink. "You, Borja, and you, Matia, you ought to think about these things once in a while." The sea was very still, with something mysterious caught among the rocks. If a drop had fallen on the surface we would have heard it. The Chink was very quiet, looking out to sea, and his hair fell to both sides of his face. He looked like one of the stained-glass figures of Santa María, and he made me vaguely afraid. He blinked and his eyes shone. He held his glasses in his right hand, and with his left he gently rubbed the bridge of his nose, where small creases formed. "Andromache, Taurus," the Chink was saying. He was naming one star after another: rosaries of stars came out of his mouth. "You ought to think about these things." The Chink's eyes, like two intent and yellow lights, were fixed on mine, amid the silence, piercing the air which hung heavily over the water. I remembered the big vault of Santa María: its darkness and also its unexpected brilliance. The Chink explained things which I almost never understood: but he knew that the figures on the stained-glass windows were his Martyrs, something like his dead brothers or relatives. And they caused him pain or reproached him. We were sitting on the ground. The almond trees covered the land, bordered at intervals with green grass, emerald green, like the sea. The almonds had already bloomed, and their black trunks stood out mysteriously against the pinkish cloud that lulled and made the light hazy, like a heavy vapor. The olive trees glistened. Their trunks formed faces, arms, mouths. The seeded earth, recently turned over, jutted out in darker squares. "My Lord," the Chink was saying, "what rich land." He seemed on the point of tears, as if the sight of it opened up a secret grief instead of giving him pleasure, as it would anyone else. Borja probably asked him something, because I heard him say: "So much kindness from God pains me." Further on, we came to the end of the Naranjal, where everything seemed asleep. We only had to reach out our hand to pick the fruit. We did not see a single keeper (we still had not reached the nursery grounds). If by chance one were around, he would be sleeping someplace, next to the irrigation tunnel, "stretched out, listening to the cool murmur of water, his eyes closed, his stick beside him." This was the image of a keeper I had formed as a child, perhaps by seeing such a portrayal in an engraving or in some story. The Naranjal was a mass of shade. We had to walk half crouching among the trees, one in front of the other. The light became dark green, in spite of a high, round sun. To the left rose the mountains, blue, grey, and sienna-colored, very beautiful and delicate. There were no woods around here, and Borja said: "And the woods, when are we going to see them?" But the Chink would not answer. He seemed to drag behind a bit, among the orange trees, until at last we dropped to the ground, exhausted. He pulled off an orange, and bit into it. He made a hole and began to suck. Shortly afterward, the juice poured down the sides of his mouth and dampened his mustache. It disgusted me. He pulled off another; its odor filled my nose, and I closed my eyes. Suddenly, I opened them and then I saw how the Chink reached out his hand and put it on Borja's leg. Half asleep, as in dreams, I saw how it slowly slipped upward, fearfully. Borja stayed still, until he brusquely moved it aside, and said: "Go away, Chink!" The odor of the oranges gave off something warm in the midst of the cold. I shuddered, lying under the trees. To the right I could see the sea, a brilliant, dark blue. From where we were lying, the earth seemed to rock gently, winding toward the beach like a spiraling rind. It was enough to make one dizzy. It seemed to form grey, curling waves. Farther on stood a group of trees, desolately bare. "They're fig trees," I thought. I remembered the one in our garden. These seemed scrubbed, with their branches gleaming under the light like metal. I stood up and left the Naranjal. I set out for a walk. Isolated houses began to appear, houses like square blocks, painted white, with small windows and reed porches. Again there were the prickly pears, the olive and carob trees. I stopped in front of a silent white house. There was a blind mule turning the water wheel. The water fell from the buckets onto the ground. The sound was peaceful and disquieting at the same time. I had gotten a good distance away from the Naranjal, walking slowly, cautiously, so as not to rouse some dog to barking. I thought about the stars. My star was ill-omened. "It's the Chink's doing. He's poisoning us with his lies about the stars, and things like that." Again, I remembered the stained-glass windows of Santa María, and I felt a pang; I did not know if it was of fear or pain. But I remembered Fermitín, a boy who had died a short time ago in the village. I never had spoken to him, but the news of his death had upset me. (I ardently desired that no one should die in the world, that all the business about death might be just one more of the many hoaxes with which men deceive children.) The sunlight came from one side, and I saw my shadow on the ground. In front of me stood the white cube of a house, almost blue under the sun, and there was my shadow on the ground, on the small plain lying toward the sea. Alone, with no trees around me, I was as still as a tree in the midst of such great solitude. Something seemed to say: "You don't understand anything, you don't ever understand . . ." I looked back, overcome by a great desire to see the orange trees, under which the Chink and Borja, and no one else, waited. (How odd, I was at the point of thinking: "And Matia is there with them, too.") As if this quiet body, with its shadow on the ground, were not mine and might be back there, between Borja and the Chink. In among the dark green foliage of the heavily laden trees shone the round fruit. The Chink was unable to look at it without getting joyful. He would say: "It's so rich." Fermitín knew it too. Every time the doctor came to see him, he asked: "And the oranges, haven't they picked them yet?" Juan Antonio's father told us that. But why think so much about Fermitín? What for? By now, he would be disintegrating under the earth. Step after step, dead men and more dead men, and for all the steps we might take, how far could we go on that island? Then I was afraid my shadow might no longer stir, as if it were the shadow of a stone. I raised my arm and I saw it darkly take shape on the ground. I heaved a big sigh, broke into a run and made for the sea. Then I walked a while before returning to the Naranjal. The pink mist of the almond trees, between the black posts of the trunks, still could not be seen. I felt a slight sinking feeling. "Olive trees, almond trees, olive trees, almond trees . . ." Everything was caught in my eyes with a blinding brilliance.)

"I already know it," I said hurriedly. And I felt my face burn. "I already know it. I don't need you to tell me anything . . . !"

"Besides, I have a letter he wrote to me, the big idiot. I've got it hidden in the iron box, and he knows it . . ."

Borja's laugh sounded low, wounding.

"He does what I order him to do . . . everything that I order."

I grabbed his hand, which was squeezing my shoulder, and pushed it away.

"Matia," he said. And his voice became more blurred. "I want you to see something I've taken from mamma. Read this, dopey! Read it, and you'll realize that you don't even know the half of it . . ."

He lit his small flashlight and showed me three letters, which were suddenly familiar to me: their color, their shape, even their odor. And then I remembered having seen them in Aunt Emilia's hands, in her pink and suffocating room. (Aunt Emilia in her folding chair, the nauseating perfume, the letters scattered on her lap. Suddenly, I thought: "They aren't letters from Uncle Álvaro . . .")

"Read these, Matia, and you'll see."

The evil light of the flashlight lit up the first sentences, the names. I looked away, I did not want to look—what we were doing was horrible—but his thin, hard thief's hands made me turn my head toward the yellowing papers, and the tiny, evil tongue of light illuminated terribly sad sentences in terribly sad returned letters (returned the same as the sea returns bodies to the shore). And I heard his voice:

"Read them, dopey, and learn something. What we're doing is bad, but I want you to know about this once and for all . . ."

It was bad to steal as we did. It was bad to torment the Chink, it was bad of Borja to dig up the residues of a sad and lost love. It was awful to be no longer innocent, to abandon Kay and Gerda, not to be even a man and a woman. But the tiny, evil tongue of light continued revealing to me, even if I did not want it to, Aunt Emilia's secret: "Jorge, my dearest . . ." "Jorge, my love . . ."

(Oh, dirty and vulgar, pathetic grownups.)

"Do you know now whom she loved? Is it clear . . . ?"

"Yours, always yours . . ." trembled Aunt Emilia's writing. (Oh, foolish, foolish grownups; and Aunt Emilia said: "I also slept with a doll, practically up until the night before my wedding.")

Poor Gorogó.

Now, I can not remember how many times I saw Manuel; nor do I remember if many days passed between encounters, or if on the contrary, they took place without respite. I can, on the other hand, exactly reconstruct the color of the earth and trees. And in my memory there is the odor of the air, the interlaced light of shadows over our heads, the dying flowers, and the well with its green resonance, beside us. The small animals of the earth fled, and at the edge of the sea, the pitas swelled proudly, like swords in a completely forgotten game.

We never made appointments at a definite hour, ever. We simply met. Manuel, who never would take a rest, nor speak with anyone, used to abandon everything to go with me. I left Borja, forgot my classes, my reading and every one of grandmother's orders. We walked side by side, we talked, or we lay on our faces, as on the first afternoon, under the trees of the Descent.

I remember that I plunged into an unfamiliar area, as into shifting waters: as if fear were overpowering me day by day. It was not the infantile terror I had suffered up until then. At times, I awoke at night and sat up startled in bed. Then I felt a lost sensation from my earliest childhood, when twilight would unnerve me and I used to think: "Night and day, night and day forever. Won't there ever be anything more?" The same confused desire came back to me: the desire that I might find, upon awakening, not merely the night and the day, but rather something new, bewildering and painful. Something like a hole through which I might escape from life.

When Borja divulged his mother's secret to me, something similar to my desire to escape from the night and the day dominated me; something as confused as the uncertain desire for justice which was beginning to take possession of my conscience.

I would have liked to slap my cousin and tell him: "No, not you, you little fake, you selfish rotter, you can't be the one . . ." Manuel was Jorge's only son, his real son.

Like a thief, I spied on Aunt Emilia when she would leave her room, in order to steal into it silently. With a vile conscience (something I did not have when helping Borja steal money) I searched for the photographs of Uncle Álvaro. He was Borja's father, he was Borja's father. I scrutinized his thin face, his too closely-set eyes, his prominent cheekbones which hurt one just to look at them. Yes, he looked like him. When my cousin forgot his mild flattering air, when Borja was alone with Juan Antonio, or Guiem, or even me, his face wore the same expression. He was (as Antonia and Lorenza would say) "a very handsome boy, too handsome to be a man." I avidly examined Borja's features, his eyes, his smile. I would tell myself it could not be, that he looked more and more like Uncle Álvaro. And I myself asked him: "Why does it matter so much to you?" and at the same time, I asked myself this question: And why, why did it matter so much to me whether Borja were or were not his son? And I sank into a heavy gloom.

I did not dare look into Aunt Emilia's eyes, and her supposed waiting for Uncle Álvaro struck me as something turbid, thick, like the perfume of her room.

Almost all the flowers were dead. Only red roses remained, and some other kinds like closed lilies, a light mauve shade. I never saw the Descent as lovely as in those days, nor the earth filled with such a perfume, even during the summer. Nevertheless, hideous things were apparently happening. At breakfast time, grandmother's newspapers rustled between her gluttonous claws, and the little cane slid to the floor again and again, like a protest. Her dull-grey ring gave off angry reflections. "'Horror upon horror, men buried alive . . .'" She would absently drink her coffee, and above her cup, her round gloomy eyes would follow the letters with morbid greediness. Sometimes Borja and I would look at the newspapers. Bombed cities, battles lost, battles won. And there, on the island, in the village, a thick and silent vengeance raged. The Taronjís climbed into their black car and scurried around the province. I remembered their cousin José Taronjí, and something caught in my throat. From that afternoon on, neither Borja nor I had returned to the *Young Simón*.

After grandmother left the wrinkled newspapers on the table, the Chink would read them in silence. Sometimes, at the sound of a door slamming, or a too sudden gust of wind, he would raise his head. Gondoliero would come to fetch him: he would perch on his shoulder, his head, his arm, or sometimes peck lightly at the edge of his ear, as if kissing it, and the Chink would pretend to read or write, smiling enigmatically.

We continued holding class in the shabby living room. The three of us at the big table, each one at a different end, separated like unacquainted chieftains. It seemed as if at both sides, steppes spread out, long regions of ice and distance separating us. It was beginning to be cold. Borja chewed the end of his fountain pen. I drew cities for Gorogó in the margins of my notebooks. Occasionally we heard Aunt Emilia playing the piano. The notes leaked downward peculiarly, as if rolling downstairs.

"What will you do, Chink, when we go off to school?" Borja asked many times.

Lauro fell silent and smiled:

"Go over your lesson, Master Borja."

Antonia said:

"Yesterday they nearly stoned Malene in the plaza."

"Why?" and both Borja and I raised our heads at the same time. A butterfly, gone astray, fluttered over Cicero's discourses.

"Just for being fresh. But the Taronjís prevented it."

"What did they do?" the Chink asked.

Mother and son exchanged glances. At that moment, Antonia was gathering up the books and notebooks and putting them to one side of the table. She brought a tray with our luncheon, and was setting out the cups. Only the sound of the cups and teaspoons could be heard.

"The crowd shaved off her hair," she said. "That's all. They took her off to the plaza of the Jews, where the boys sometimes make bonfires, and the women cut off her hair. They made an example of her."

My hands trembled on the table, so that I hid them. I felt like a coward, wretched, and I felt like saying: "Manuel is my friend, he held Gorogó in his hands, and he didn't even ask what good a doll like that was."

The stairs creaked, and Antonia hurried out of the room. Grandmother was coming down the stairs, clumsily. She came in almost immediately, followed by Antonia, and stood next to the door, looking at us. As we stood up, there fell to the floor, over by the Chink, a pile of books and an impertinent yellow pencil which rolled as far as grandmother's feet (small feet, her flesh squeezing out of the shoes). She came forward, bent at the waist, her knees thrust out, muttering broken phrases. It was the first time grandmother had entered that room, the first time she had interrupted our classes. Grandmother stared coldly at Lauro.

"Let it go," she interrupted. "What happened with that woman?"

Antonia, who was quiet and erect, standing at one side, blinked:

"Señora, that woman . . . it seems she was insolent with the Taronjís. She showed herself . . . not very resigned. She's a bad woman, Señora, and they've taught her a lesson."

"What lesson?"

"They shaved off her hair. You'll remember, she had a beautiful head of gold hair . . ."

"Red hair," grandmother corrected. "Yes, I remember it. It wasn't gold, it was red."

She threw the newspaper on the table.

"Here, a head of hair is shaven, there, this other thing is done."

We timidly looked at the newspaper photograph. The photograph showed people hung somewhere or other. But it was so blurred that it came out hideously bloody, macabre. And I thought of the straw doll Guiem's gang brandished at the bonfires to demonstrate their victory

over us. The same shapeless doll, dressed in a ragged
sweater, which Borja managed to recover at the cost of a
large rip in his arm.

Firmly and heavily, with her stupid little cane in her
hand, grandmother went out. The Chink quickly
grabbed the newspaper, and unfolded it. In big headlines was the news that in a village on the peninsula the
parish priest had been thrown to the hogs. For a moment,
I visualized Monsignor Mayol, fighting with a herd of
pigs: possibly the same kind that were so abundant on
the island: fierce animals, with long eyeteeth. I could
not help it: the pigs with their eyeteeth smiled exactly
like grandmother, Borja, and probably me.

"Son, you have to eat," Antonia said.

For the second time we were hearing that word. "She
calls him that," I thought, "since she knows they are
going to turn him out."

I felt Borja's eyes on me and I turned to look at him.
In the way he knit his brows, in the way he bit his lips,
even in the black, shiny curl which fell on his forehead,
I guessed what he was going to say to me:

"Matia, let's go."

The Chink opened his mouth and closed it again.
Then, he sat down, with his head bowed, and folded
the newspaper. Antonia, opaque, as if she had no soul,
poured the coffee into the cups.

"Where?" I asked him, hardly out of the room. It was
cold, and I pulled my jacket around me, holding it with
my hands. I was afraid of what he was going to answer.

"To see Manuel."

"No, Borja, no!"

I tried to hold him back by the sleeve, but he got away. He set off at a run, ahead of me. His delicate, golden legs jumped over the walls around the Descent. There was a full, ripe sun that afternoon. A golden season was beginning, and it had its own special light, a red and mauve glow among the trees. A warm sun, like an old wine, that had to be swallowed in sips so it might not go to one's head. We were at the beginning of October.

Borja stopped at Manuel's door, as I had that afternoon, before Manuel turned to ask me to wait for him. I contemplated the hollow in the nape of his neck, and I looked at him and hoped he would not call Manuel.

Through the open door we could see the olive trees and the well in which the dead dog was thrown. The sky, I told myself, was the same as then and as it always was; only on earth did things change. Now it was bathed by the glowing light of a ripe, late sun. It was perhaps five in the afternoon.

Borja continued gazing toward the olive trees, but Manuel was not there.

"Where is that guy at this time of day?" he asked. There was great passion in his voice, and his agitation was obvious.

"I don't know."

Impatient, he lifted his shoulders, and repeated:

"Where is he, Matia, where is he? You'll be sorry if you don't tell me . . ."

"I swear I don't know . . ."

"But where do you two meet?"

It was useless to tell him that we did not meet in any set way, and it was useless to explain to him (and neither could he have known) how we would just happen upon one another without understanding or thinking about it. It was useless to give him any other explanation. I became terrified when I remembered the day Manuel was about to say: "Stop there, this is my world. Stop, this is the private door of my kingdom." I was terrified to see that Borja, brazen and bold ("wicked, wicked Borja"), shrugged his shoulders and crossed that door for the first time. That door was the barricade, the dark sanctuary to something which was beyond my possible love. I watched him with an anguished heart, and leaned against the trunk of the first olive tree. The thick summer greenness had already withered. In among the trees I saw the well, covered with moss and rust, like a mysterious eye in the earth.

The house had a small arched porch. The little outdoor lamp seemed broken, as if it had been stoned. There was a profound silence, in which two golden bees chased one another. The pink veil of sun bathed everything, as in a dream. And there was a thick fragrance, sweet as the sugar of flowers or of must. One of grandmother's pigeons, a dark grey one, was pecking on the first step, next to a puddle.

"Manuel . . ." Borja called.

The shadows were stirring on the ground. In large clay pots the intense red of the geraniums was gleaming. Everything glowed, as if a golden rain, light and glimmering, had fallen. The glass of the window on the right side mirrored blue and green. The balcony was open and there was a throbbing in the profound silence, as if everyone were asleep or enchanted. The orchard seemed freshly watered.

"Manuel!" Borja cried again, more vehemently.

The pigeon rose in flight, crossed over our heads and perched on the wall. Its shadow on the ground, as seen from the olive tree against which I was leaning, contained something magical. Its wings were moving along the earth. "Everything in the world is so mysterious," I thought.

Manuel arrived at that moment. He was very serious, spattered with clay, and barefoot. He leaned up against the wall, and slowly, without looking at us, began to put on his sandals. The shadow of his long eyelashes, stubbornly lowered, darkened against his face. He was much taller than Borja; he could have crushed him.

"Manuel," my cousin said violently. "I've come to ask you something: Whose side are you on, Guiem's or mine?"

Manuel stared at him, and for the first time, I detected a fleeting tremor of anger in him. An anger as deep and as painful as his sadness.

"I don't understand," he said.

Borja came closer. I could see he was trembling, holding himself back:

"Come on with me! We're going to Son Major!"

For the first time that afternoon, Manuel turned to me. Borja interruped:

"Come on! Come on, if you don't want something to happen to you . . . Something worse than what happened to your mother."

I wished he had never said that. I felt it like a slap. But I was scared of my own cowardliness. Manuel's dark skin tinged a reddish shade, from his forehead to his neck.

"I have work," he answered.

Borja looked at me:

"Tell him to come, Matia."

Before I could open my mouth—and I was aware of a burning fire rushing over my forehead, ears and neck—Manuel raised his right hand, which glistened, and said:

"Don't say anything, Matia, you don't need . . ."

I turned my eyes away from his, and he himself began the expedition.

First we went to get Juan Antonio, who looked out over the balcony when he heard our whistle. He was chewing something, probably having a snack. He came down quickly and took his place at Manuel's side. They continued walking, one beside the other, and I behind. It really looked as if he were being led away like a prisoner. Manuel walked slowly, his arms heavy on either side of his body.

We were already leaving the village when the cripple saw us.

"Now he'll go and tell the others . . ." Juan Antonio said in a rush.

León and Carlos were studying, but they came out immediately when they heard us.

The road that went to Son Major wound upward little by little above the village, as far as the big twist in the mountain, over the cliff. The sun glared down full along the road, as upon a blank wall.

When we reached Son Major, we stopped, intimidated. We might have limited ourselves to stopping there (as Manuel and I sometimes did), pressed against the wall, looking at each other, listening to the wind; but on that particular day, Sanamo was walking along behind the iron gate and he immediately caught sight of Manuel. Upon seeing him, he opened his mouth and raised his arms to the sky. But not a single word came out of his mouth. Laughing his malign laugh, he came closer up to the iron gate, making the keys jingle in his hands.

"Manuel, Manuel, my little boy!" he cried out of his toothless mouth, while he drew the creaking door latch. Sanamo's hair, long and grey, waved in the wind.

Manuel, with his prisoner's air, which irritated me, stood quietly in front of the iron gate, his head slightly lowered. He was taller than all of us, even taller than I, the tallest of the group. There he was, strangely brilliant in the afternoon sun, which was already disappearing, all the gold of the sun trapped in his dark skin, his reddish hair. Sanamo stared at him, as if entranced. Borja, holding on to the heavy bars of the iron gate with both hands, was smiling and trying to be amiable, as when he would ask grandmother for something.

"Hello, Sanamo," he said, with false cheerfulness, "can we pay a visit to Don Jorge?"

Sanamo looked at him shrewdly and smiled evilly. He

opened the iron gate wide, as if a coach were passing through, instead of a terrified group of children.

"Come in," he said. "The master will be delighted to receive such handsome young people."

Manuel remained as if nailed to the ground, and Borja pushed him brusquely inside.

At last, the garden of Son Major appeared before us. It was very shady because of the high walls. The wind always blew there, and the palm trees rocked. The steps that went up to the house seemed covered with a lizard-green moss. The house was handsome, with a long loggia of white arches and windows painted blue, but it was very old and run-down. Around the upper part of the wall climbed a thick vine which gave it a damp and somber appearance. On the left grew the magnolias, no longer in bloom. But there was an unusual perfume in the air: of other flowers, other shadows, and other echoes, which one could scarcely identify, and hardly dared divine. The earth and all the leaves seemed to have just been watered.

3

I shall always remember the rosy light in which everything seemed steeped, as in a marvelously golden wine. Even if the magnolias were no longer in bloom and the flowers were dying—except for the red roses, so dark and deep they seemed black, like dried, but still fresh, shuddering blood—the whole atmosphere was permeated by a poignant aroma. Sanamo went to the inner garden, and soon returned laughing, as if something weirdly wonderful had occurred:

"Come in, children, come in."

He shook from head to feet with an absurd and wild happiness. Something seemed to clutch at our feet and voices; no one went forward or said anything. Borja's blustering left him, and Juan Antonio, Carlos and León seemed trapped in their sullen timidity. We looked just as Sanamo said we did (probably to humiliate us): a group of ridiculous, hysterical children who imagined that being received by Jorge of Son Major was a bold adventure.

"Let's go, my darlings, let's go. What are you waiting for? The master is inviting you to have a snack with him," Sanamo was saying, writhing with laughter (just like the old Troll of Dovre, crowned with icicles and pine cones, when the Seventh Little Princess of the Hill of the Elves took him by the hand).

Only Manuel recovered his composure. He took me by the hand and we followed the jingling keys of the old man of the garnet-red rose. Behind us crunched the fine sand of the garden under the footsteps of Borja, Juan Antonio, Carlos, and León.

Jorge of Son Major was seated at the end of the garden, overwhelmed by dark roses. (The garden, as if steeped in wine; the high walls separating it from the world, as if pressed onto the rough mountain side.) There were cherry trees, another magnolia, and the famous grape arbor, a source of envy to the mayor's wife and to my own grandmother. The grape clusters, pale blue to violet, hung from the pergola. A long table stood under the arbor. The sun turned a bottle a glowing, transparent pink. It looked like a lamp. Jorge of Son Major, seated behind the table, appeared cut off at the waist, like the bust of an odd saint. There was a burst of the last light of day. Manuel drew me gently by the hand, and we came closer up to him. I cannot remember what he told us, I only know that his smile and voice were as distant to us as his legend. His somber eyes, with their bluish corneas, like Manuel's, were looking at us wearily.

With his right hand, he motioned us to sit down at the table. His hair was grey, almost white, and luxuriant. His skin was dark, almost as dark as the nape of Manuel's neck, and he wore a threadbare mariner's jacket with gilded buttons. His hands were large, rough, slow-moving. On the whole he seemed a sad man, as if out of place. One by one, he spoke to us. First to Borja and then to me, treating us as real children. Borja was burning, tense, trying to stretch himself up as much as possible in order to appear the tallest. Jorge asked after grandmother. (I thought: "No one ever asks about my father.") Jorge, seated behind the table, insisted we come nearer to him, as if he were a bishop or an irascible prince. Manuel's hand and mine seemed impossible to separate. I do not know which one of us tightened our interlaced fingers harder; perhaps both of us at once, as if we wanted to take hold of something out of our suddenly awakened solitude.

Jorge rested his hand on my shoulder and stared intently at our linked fingers. Not until that moment did

Jorge's eyes seem to look so much like Manuel's. I felt the weight of his hand, and his touch awoke a strange feeling in me. Something held me, motionless, as if I were incapable of separating myself from his touch. Jorge's hand wafted a rare aroma of cedar (I suddenly thought of the box of Cuban cigars that my father forgot someplace in the country house, and which I, as a child, sniffed delightedly). It seemed as if the fragrance spread through the air: the grape clusters, the sun, the wine, all exhaled it. Or perhaps it was not his hand; perhaps it was only the dream which saturated the hidden garden of Son Major.

"And you," he said, "are you María Teresa's daughter?"

I realized that my smile was forced.

"You don't look like her. No, you don't look anything like her."

Perhaps his saying it hurt me. Or perhaps precisely the opposite happened: it delighted me a great deal to hear it.

"I'm going to have excellent company this afternoon . . . Sanamo!"

He ordered him to bring more wine and glasses. Sanamo obeyed, and added almonds, cheese, and slices of dark, salted bread, very different from the tasteless bread of the island.

"Sanamo kneads this bread, in the style of some country of his acquaintance," said Jorge. And his laugh was maliciously answered by the old devil who served him.

We did not understand, and it disturbed us that they laughed every time they looked at each other.

A fluttering of wings shook the garden, as if someone might have been beating against metal. Grandmother's grey, white and black pigeons flew over the walls into the garden. Their obscure shadows crossed the ground, and Jorge pointed them out with his hand:

"Look: Doña Práxedes' pigeons."

Sanamo left the wine on the table. Jorge added:

"The pigeons come to my house, and my white rooster, according to Sanamo, has a preference for the fig tree in your garden . . . Isn't that so, Borja?"

Borja nodded, smiling. Jorge turned to Manuel for the first time. Our eyes were fixed on him. Jorge said:

"Sit here, at my right. And you, young lady, at my other side."

He gently separated our hands and raised Manuel above all of us, even in the tone of voice which he used in speaking to him. I looked at Borja, who was waiting for that moment only. ("He's destroyed," I told myself.) It seemed to me my cousin was about to say something. He reddened, and the glitter of his eyes made me think that what he most wished might possibly be true: it was the same wild glitter of Jorge's eyes. I was afraid he would pounce on Manuel, that he might push him and throw him out of there, just to seat himself to the right of his idol. Jorge spoke, as if unaware of the pain he had just given my cousin:

"And Lauro? Where have you all left him?"

Our laughter stifled the moment. It seemed as if the mere mention of the Chink caused all our timidity to vanish. Only Borja was left bursting with anxiety and humiliation, his lips trembling. Manuel remained silent, as if looking inside himself, as if unaware of the distinction Jorge bestowed upon him. He was even the only one whom Jorge did not caress.

Jorge himself poured wine for us, and he served Manuel first. We all began to talk. Even Juan Antonio, so serious and reticent, laughed and asked questions.

Twice again, Jorge ordered Sanamo to bring wine. Jorge's arm was around my shoulders, and I hardly dared to move. I could scarcely sense anything beyond the light from the bottle, that bottle like an illuminated, pomegranate-colored lamp; above all, that unusual pressure, so strange to my shoulders, astonished me, and I became, before my own eyes, an unfamiliar creature.

Perhaps we were hoping he would tell us important things. I do not know. But we were actually the ones who talked to him. One by one we were relieved of our words. And he did not tell us anything about the Greek islands, nor the *Delfín,* while we told him about the battles between the two gangs, our secret trips to Mariné's café . . .

"Ah yes, yes . . ." he said, as if remembering something very far off. "Now I remember Mariné. Tell him to come and see me some day."

Sanamo grimaced, muttering.

We did not know how, but a long time passed. The sun slid behind the walls. Jorge remained at the end of the table, with Manuel and me at either side of him. Manuel and I, face to face, and separated by the table, were gazing at one another. Manuel was the only one silent. He ate slowly, biting the brown bread as if against his will, pulling each grape from the cluster one by one with his dark, scratched hands. The grapes glistened between his fingers. Senselessly, I stopped looking at him to look at Jorge, and something occurred to me, something so new and painful . . . Jorge was not as we imagined him. He was neither a god, nor the wind, nor the wild and savage hurricane of which Mariné, the Chink, and even Borja spoke. Jorge of Son Major was a tired, sad man, whose sadness and solitude were magnetic. Seeing him, hearing him speak, looking at his almost white hair, I felt that I loved his weariness and his sadness as I never had loved anything. Perhaps because he possessed everything I wished for. The hurried flight, the grief for Kay and Gerda, for Peter Pan and the Little Mermaid, seemed to me over and done with. For I found in Jorge's weariness something like a return toward a place I could not even name. To see him there, in his threadbare mariner's jacket, surrounded by the walled garden, taking refuge in the dark roses, in his memories, made me want to reach out, drink those memories, swallow his sadness ("thanks, thanks, for your sadness"), to take shelter in it, flee, like him, and be sunk forever in the large glass of rosé wine of his nostalgia, which filled me magically. To be with him among the scattered ashes of the *Delfín,* watering flowers. "This," I told myself, "is perhaps what grownups call love." I could not know, as I never had loved anyone. I did not dare move and have his arm slip from around my shoulders: I could not lose that arm, as if it were the only thing that linked me to life. I was dazzled by his already full life, and perhaps by his absence of hope.

Probably the only thing he was waiting for was the visit of the Black Lady, and I (poor me, an insignificant creature of fourteen empty years, how would I be able to let him know I was no longer like Kay and Gerda?), perhaps I could serve him as a little corpse. Hopeless, I was looking at his white hair and I thought his heart, enclosed behind the old blue jacket, must be like a mountain of ashes, like the *Delfín*. If I could encompass his sadness and weariness, take possession of them like a little thief! and an intense pain overcame me, as well as a desperate and terrible love such as I have never felt again. Manuel's words: *"That I love him a great deal,"* hurt me, and buzzed about my forehead like bees. The words astonished me, too.

A rain, so light that at first we did not notice it, began to fall. We were all talking, and we seemed very happy, but perhaps we were not happy, neither Borja, Manuel, nor I. (Mariné told us: "He has no other sickness but his old age, but that's serious.") He was not old yet, as I was not a woman yet: he still had not abandoned life, as I still had not entered it. I kept repeating this while I brought the wine glass to my lips again and again. We were all drinking, and Jorge was laughing at what we told him. He spoke only from time to time. He poured more wine in our glasses, and looked at us, especially at Manuel and me. And in the middle of our stupid uproar, our foolish questions and explanations, how far away, and even more, how alone he was. And I said to myself: "He's much more alone here, among us, than when he's with his roses and pigeons." He did not believe in anything, and I still had to believe in something. I said to myself: "Just like when I was a little girl and I thought: *Death is not real. They tell it to us children to fool us.*" (And I remembered when I would put myself halfway into the wardrobe, with my atlas open in the shadows, and would look at the archipelago and would stare, enchanted at every name: Lēmnos, Chios, Àndros, Sériphos . . . Kýthnos, Mýkonos, Polýgyros, Náxos, Anáphē, Psára . . . Ah, yes, names and more names, like the wind and dreams. Dreamily, I would run my finger around in a circle on the blue glossy paper, from Corfu to Mytilene. And the words, like a music: *He sailed on the* Delfín, *he lived on it, and he scarcely walked the earth: he went as far as Asia Minor . . .*)

Sanamo appeared, bringing his guitar. Jorge said:

"Let's go to the porch, Sanamo."

Surprised, we saw how Sanamo and Manuel—with practiced gesture—picked him up under the arms and helped him to the porch. I looked at his back, his legs which hardly obeyed him. At that moment, Juan Antonio whispered in my ear:

"He's half paralyzed . . . don't you see? My father says so: he's getting paralyzed, little by little, and will end up by not being able to move. And as soon as it reaches his head . . . paf! That's it."

Juan Antonio seemed to relish these words. His teeth

and lips were stained with wine and the juice of purple grapes. Between Manuel's and Sanamo's efforts, Jorge was seated on a bench under the enclosed porch. We all ran to take refuge there because the rain was falling heavily now. Over our heads, with the sudden flight of the pigeons—unexpected forms in that dying light—the bells of Santa María rang out. We surrounded Jorge, and I kneeled at his feet. I expect the wine had gone to everyone's head. Juan Antonio, León and Borja were talking almost simultaneously. Jorge and Sanamo were looking at each other, and suddenly Jorge said:

"Getting children drunk is uproariously entertaining!"

Sanamo let out a hoarse guffaw, and began to strum his guitar. Everything was invaded with a wild, red gaiety, overflowing from the vigorous rain which fell on us from the sky like a scream. Sanamo's melody was as intense as the red roses. Sanamo said:

"Youngsters, join in . . ."

Borja was hoarse, and Juan Antonio, and everyone—except Manuel—tried to follow the song, but we would get mixed up and have to start over again.

"Is it Andalusian?" asked León.

"No."

"Is it Italian?"

"No, no . . ."

He did not want to say what country the music he interpreted was from, just as he did not like to say where he was born.

Still kneeling next to him, I raised my head toward

Jorge. But how could his glance cause so much pain?
I undid my braid, which slid over the nape of my neck,
and for a moment I felt his fingers grazing my skin. He
wanted to braid it again, but he did not know how. I
saw the glints of light in my hair, as I shook it out, and I
heard him say:

"How strange! It's not black, it's almost red . . ."

He gathered a lock between his fingers and looked at it
against the sun. It seemed as if all that was happening in
some dark episode of my memory. All the things in the
garden—rose, gold and scarlet, my hair between his
fingers, miraculously turned tawny-colored.

He let his hand fall on my wrist and closed it. He said
dryly:

"These hands were joined."

His other hand grasped Manuel's wrist and brought it
close to mine, in spite of the fact that both of us were
resisting, as if frightened. Manuel half-closed his eyes.
Something glistened on his eyelashes, perhaps the rain.
He was serious, as if grief-stricken. Jorge added:

"Like that."

And he joined our hands. I raised my eyes and met
Borja's, flaming. Without being able to control himself,
he came up to us and tried with his fists to separate our
hands, which were once again intertwined. Roughly,
Jorge drove Borja away. And even though he was laughing, there was something cruel in his look.

Borja remained quiet, his shoulders drooping a little.
He backed so far away that he was outside the protection

of the porch, and the rain fell over his forehead and cheeks, without his even noticing it. He looked at San Jorge in a way the others could never understand. (I, yes, my poor friend, yes, I understood you and felt sorry for you.) He tried to smile, but his lips quivered, and again he sought shelter on the porch, humiliated in a way no one had ever seen him before. Juan Antonio and the administrator's boys seemed to be looking at us, Manuel and me, enviously. And I said to myself: "How is it possible that all of us are in love with him?" And I hated Sanamo's guitar, which poisoned us. Every time Manuel and I wanted to separate our hands, Jorge put his on top of mine and prevented it.

Borja sat down, his elbows on his knees and his face between his hands. We did not know if he was crying or laughing, or simply if his head was aching from so much drinking.

Sanamo's guitar music could be heard, and the noise of the rain, which was dying down. Everything was glowing pallidly, in trembling drops: the green, blue and gold clusters of grapes, the magnolia leaves, the October roses.

Then, Jorge said:

"Do you know what, children? Don't think that at the point of death you'll remember great deeds or important events that have happened to you. Don't think you'll remember big adventures, or even happy moments you could still live. Only things like this: an afternoon like this one, some glasses of wine, some roses covered with rain."

(While we were at Son Major, Guiem and his gang had built bonfires in the plaza of the Jews, and burned three figures made of old rags: Borja, Manuel, and me. The Chink told us later.)

THE *WHITE COCK*

GRANDMOTHER found out.

"Why did you go to Son Major?"

She remained seated on her rocking chair, stuffing pills to calm her into her mouth. Her voice sounded quiet and steady, as usual, but it seemed to me she was furious. Her grey eyes stared at us intently. We could not see Aunt Emilia's face; she was seated next to the balcony, with her back to us. The night was humid and full of odors. Borja and I felt dizzy. As in a dream I feared or believed I saw grandmother's head detach itself and rise, just like a balloon floating toward the ceiling, grimacing oddly. Grandmother's eyes, like two tentacled fish, observed us crudely.

Her dark mouth engulfed the pills from the brown flask: one, a sip of water, two, another sip of water.

Antonia was waiting to serve supper, her hands crossed over her apron, and Gondoliero, wildly blue, flew toward her head.

"Answer me, Borja," grandmother insisted.

Borja tried to smile, but he rocked too much on his feet:

"Grandmother . . ." he began to say. And he remained silent, smiling stupidly.

"Come here."

Borja came closer and grandmother put her nose to his face, as she did with me when she suspected me of smoking.

"He's given you wine . . . I imagined as much. Just like him to give wine to children! He must have had a good laugh at all of you, amusing himself at your expense."

I concentrated on the trembling of the Chink's hands.

"You, Lauro, were you present?"

The Chink opened his mouth twice, and Borja took over:

"Yes, grandmother, he came with us; he couldn't do anything else but come!"

His laugh rang false. Grandmother was looking at the Chink, her eyes like two big-clawed crabs turning back toward some strange beach.

"Señora . . . the children . . ."

Grandmother raised her right hand, indicating that the conversation was over.

We went to the dining room and ate in silence. I hardly could swallow the food; it was torture. I do not know what was happening to Borja, but I felt sick, upset. My head hurt a great deal, and an enormous drowsiness was overcoming me. I could not avoid seeing strange things: suddenly, grandmother's big white wave of hair rose over her forehead and dissolved in foam, and her hand came loose from her body, jumping over the tablecloth like Antonia's blue parakeet. On the other hand, I could not look toward Aunt Emilia; something prevented my raising my eyes to her.

The supper scarcely over, grandmother had us kiss her hand and cheek. When I went to take leave of Aunt Emilia, she looked at me intently with her little pinky eyes.

"Matia," she said in a low voice. "Matia . . ."

I felt completely sleepy, lethargic, and singularly irritable toward everyone.

"Matia," Aunt Emilia went on. Perhaps she was saying something else, but I did not understand her. Everything was going around in circles. I hung on to the arm of the chair firmly. She got up.

It seems to me she began to talk, to repeat her eternal song: that I was sick, or something like that. Antonia wanted to carry me to bed, but Aunt Emilia prevented it. She put her arm around my waist, and helped me up the staircase.

I believe I remember, confusedly enough, that she undressed me and helped me to bed. I remember the feeling of great relief as I slid between the coolness of the sheets, and how my head seemed to spin, colliding against the walls of the room, while she was looking at me.

"Sleep," she said, in her gentle voice.

It seems to me I tried to get up a couple of times, and

she stopped me. Then the door creaked and I heard grandmother's footsteps. "The big beast," I thought, recalling Borja's expressions. I looked, with half-closed eyes: the door hurled a square of yellow light along the floor. The shadow of grandmother and her little bamboo cane were quiveringly outlined on the floor. I felt a great weight on my eyelids. Aunt Emilia got up hurriedly, whispering something to her:

"She's sick, mamma . . . I told you before. This child has something, she's not like other children . . ."

Grandmother pushed her aside and came up to my bed. I closed my eyes solidly and squeezed my eyelids. Grandmother said with her usual hardness:

"Don't be stupid, Emilia. She's absolutely the same as all girls. Only she's drunk, that's all."

Aunt Emilia weakly tried to defend us. And all at once, it seemed to me she began to cry. She wept quietly, like a little girl. It was painful and astonishing to hear her. Grandmother said:

"It doesn't seem possible, Emilia, it just doesn't seem possible . . . You still haven't forgotten? Can't you see he's a boor . . . willful and embittered? Don't you realize he's a poor man, sick and alone? That's enough of that fantasy, please! Forget these childish things. You're a woman, with your husband at the front and a fifteen-year-old son. Emilia, Emilia . . . !"

She repeated her name, but there was no compassion in her voice. Then she left, and I heard how the tic-tac of her little bamboo cane went off in the distance.

When Aunt Emilia left and I was alone in the dark, the sleepiness had disappeared and I was very thirsty. The pain in my head persisted, and a cold sweat covered me. Clumsily, I got up and went to open the window. The night air entered, and so did the breeze from the sea which breathed deeply at the bottom of the Descent. The air stunned me, and I was on the verge of falling to the floor.

When I returned to bed, a peculiar noise caused me to sit up again. The door opened slowly and I recognized Borja's silhouette. As soon as he closed the door behind him, he ran toward me like an avalanche. He sat down on the edge of the bed and lit the night-table lamp: a red glass lampshade, which lit up like a wrathful eye. I covered my face with my hands, but he pulled them off, furiously:

"You pervert," he said. (And because of the way in which he said it, I guessed he must have been thinking of that word a long time, before coming to hurl it at me.) "At fourteen, in love with a man of fifty!"

With trembling fingers, he lit a cigarette. The little package stuck out of his pajama pocket. He exhaled a couple of puffs of smoke, striking the attitude he used when he wanted to intimidate me. But the cigarette quivered between his lips. The smoke came out in two columns through the holes of his nose, like two long eye-teeth.

"You're worse," I answered. "You're more perverted, because you're a boy, and also . . ."

204)

He spit his cigarette onto the floor and crushed it out
against the rug. ("And tomorrow, you devil, they'll think
it was I who did that.") With our arms entwined, we
fell to the floor, and in the struggle I hit my head against
the foot of the bed. My forehead between my hands,
tightening my lips in order not to groan, I sat down.
Everything was spinning around me. My hair spread out
(I remember that it came close to my waistline), and
tangled between my fingers. I felt very excited, and yet
it was not possible to laugh or cry about him.

"Get in bed, you idiot," he said. "Get off the floor at
once."

I obeyed him. My head hurt and I wanted to vomit. I
was hoping he would leave me in peace, and let me sleep.
But he remained there, the little monster.

"You're not going to forget what happened this afternoon," he said.

He lit a cigarette again. Before he could stop me, I
grabbed the package from him and put it under my
pillow. He raised his hand over me, closed his fist, and
biting his lips with anger, let it fall heavily upon the bedspread. Then he looked at me so sadly that I was touched.
I caressed his hair, as if he were still a little boy, and he
shrugged his shoulders lightly, half-closing his eyes. In
his turn, he picked up a lock of my hair and twisted it
between his fingers, gently, as he had done so many times
on the loggia.

"Matia, Matia . . ." he said very softly.

Suddenly he moved away from me and went toward
the door. He looked like a goblin. Behind a slight creak-

ing of wood, he disappeared. Stretching my hand toward the night table I turned off the light. Darkness absorbed everything, and I do not remember anything more.

I woke up face down, across the bed. My head still hurt a great deal. The bedspread and part of the sheets—as almost every morning—were on the floor. On my shoulders, I felt the tiny feet of little Gondoliero, who pecked softly at my ear. Antonia, as usual, was putting things in order. I felt the heat of the sun on the back of my neck. "Today will be a bright, awful day, I'll walk around here with my eyes closed, going mad every time a door is banged." The phantoms returned immediately and I grabbed the pillow to take refuge underneath it, telling myself: "Jorge. He's horrible. I'll never go back to Son Major." The phantoms came in a rush along with the hangover from the wine, seating themselves on the canopy of the bed, sticking their octopus fingers under the pillow, and tickling my recollections. Everything from the previous afternoon, even the memory of the flowers, hurt like a slanderous attack. "Oh Jorge, oh poor Aunt Emilia." Hysterically, I felt sorry for that woman whom I did not love in my whole life.

"Miss Matia, it's nine o'clock," I heard Antonia say.

Her velvety feet scarcely grazed the rug, like moles. ("They're like poor Thumbelina's mole, the hideous mole who wanted to marry her.") I opened my right eye.

"Tell your disgusting Gondoliero to get out of here," I said hoarsely.

Antonia whistled gratingly, as if in a whisper, and it hurt inside and outside of my ears. I let out a groan, and Gondoliero fled to her shoulder, like a wandering flower.

"The bath is ready, Miss Matia . . ."

I screamed, groaned, protested. Antonia was quiet. I let myself fall on the rug, with the idiotic gesture of a spoiled child, and opened my eyes.

It was a horrible grey day, luminous, glowing like aluminum. The sun penetrated the transparent skin of the sky, like a swollen burn. Everything was shining, with a nervous, metallic brilliance.

"It's going to rain," I complained. "Isn't it so, Antonia, isn't it going to rain?"

Antonia poured warm water in the rudimentary bathtub, and everything was covered with steam. My voice was drowned out.

When I went down to breakfast, grandmother found that I was pale, with rings under my eyes, and that my hair was hideously combed.

"You're almost fifteen. It seems incredible, Matia, how you look!"

The newspapers with their blue wrappers were lying in wait. I read sideways: "The troops of General . . ." Borja was finishing his cocoa, and the Chink was waiting in the study room, behind the notebooks ("How awful, now: declensions, Latin verbs!").

"When will we go to school?" Borja asked. "I'd like it so much. This village is getting to be a bore!"

"I'm glad you want to go to school," answered grandmother. "You'll go, both of you, after Christmas . . . Come here, Matia."

I came up to her as slowly as it was possible without incurring her anger.

"Get over here!"

She took my head between her two bony hands, and I felt her diamond nail itself into my right cheek. She was using a horrible cologne which was supposed to be fresh and rustic, but was medicinal instead. I felt her eyes on mine, physically, like two ants racing across my pupils, my painful cornea.

"What's happening to you?" she asked, like a bite.

I could not stand any more, and I cried:

"And Borja, what's happening to him? Do I always have to be the worst?"

"What's happening to you, I said?" she insisted coldly.

She shoved me by my arm.

"I don't like daydreaming. I don't usually waste my time."

"Your time," I said to myself. And I looked at her, hoping she might read what I was thinking in my eyes: "Your useless and wicked time, you can't waste that!"

"Matia," she went on, "what happened yesterday had better not happen again. And you, Borja, listen carefully: you'll both be pardoned this time, because perhaps you didn't know . . . But from now on it's absolutely forbidden to go to Son Major. And don't let me hear of you exchanging one word more with that degenerate Sanamo!"

"No, grandmother." My cousin bent his head. He

kissed grandmother's hand and she grazed his cheek with the tips of her fingers.

We left the room, leaving the door open and then stopping behind it, to listen to what they would say. (Borja taught me this trick the first day I set foot in the house.)

Grandmother said:

"You know, Emilia, with these children we have to be a bit indulgent. They haven't known good times: this disaster, the war . . . I, at Matia's age, already had four or five suitors! But they live in such an unsettled epoch . . . Everything is becoming strange around us! I think they need school soon, and that's what they'll have."

"Mother"—Aunt Emilia's voice seemed far off—"Matia is not a girl like other girls . . . Remember, mother: María Teresa began like that. Antonia says she screams at night . . ."

"These children drink," grandmother said. "I am sure they drink. There is someone that provides them with alcohol and cigarettes, that's all. They're at a difficult age, and these are bad times. Antonia, bring me the pills."

Borja and I exchanged glances. He was very serious, and for the first time I thought: he is not a child. (He was not a man, no. But he was no longer a boy.)

2

I scarcely know how winter came. Or perhaps it still was not properly winter, but I remember that it got cold.

Up from the sea, over the Descent, the greenish, humid cold came creeping. The black tree trunks against the golden haze which stretched from the cliff seemed like melancholy, sinister creatures, nailed behind the house, manifestations of silent protest. The light turned green and silver around the leaves of the olive trees. The pigeons fled over the almond groves, toward Son Major or Manuel's orchards. Sometimes, their cooing under the window awoke me. The living room fireplace had already been lit, and at night, Antonia warmed the sheets with a small copper brazier, filled with embers. The butterflies, the bees, and most of the birds—except for the gulls, like spread-out streamers which formed white fringes along the edge of the sea—all disappeared. Borja and I put on thick, crepe-soled shoes instead of sandals, and Antonia took woolen clothes, still impregnated with the odor of mothballs, out of the chests. When we tried on our sweaters, grandmother observed that we had grown too much that summer: they were tight under the arms and the sleeves scarcely came down to our wrists. One day Aunt Emilia took us to the city and fitted us out from head to toe. Borja, in his long grey flannel pants, looked like a man. It struck me as very strange not to see his golden bare legs, almost without fuzz, coming out of his blue pants worn out in the seat, short or rolled up over his knees. My detestable white pleated skirts and sleeve-less blouses were replaced by some pleated skirts of Scotch wool, and itchy, long-sleeved, closed-neck sweaters, no less detestable. I fought against putting on stockings, and Aunt Emilia bought me some long English-knit socks

—"Sport-type, lovely!" she said—with hideous green, grey, and yellow diamond shapes. They cut off my braids and let me wear my hair straight, hardly touching my shoulders, pulled toward the back with a black velvet ribbon intervening, which turned me into a somewhat suspicious Alice in Wonderland. When grandmother gave us her approval, she again began to complain of the swift passage of time and to yearn for the inimitable sailor middies. But it seems to me that they never mattered to her at all—neither the flight of time, nor even less the overexaggerated sailor outfits in which Borja was photographed as a child, a parody of the son of the last Tsar, preserved in an album by Aunt Emilia.

Sometimes, Manuel worked in the orchard. I knew, through Antonia, that he asked for work in the village and was denied it. On occasion, he was accompanied by his younger brother and sister: a boy of eleven and a girl of nine, redheaded like Malene, thin and sad, who did not go to school. Sometimes I saw Manuel seated on the steps of his porch, a child on either side of him, showing them an old atlas similar to mine. I remember the sound of his voice explaining geography to them. I looked over the wall of his orchard, and I heard him pronounce names: "Caucasus," "Mount Athos," "Asia Minor." It touched me to know he was following my routes ("just like me, inside the wardrobe"). I remember his words very well, one morning, under a cold sun: the three of them were seated, on the porch or under the olive trees. Suddenly, the little boy or girl would whisper: "Matia is there behind the wall!" Then Manuel would turn his head and look at me.

On more than one occasion we walked together across the rocks, searching for limpets, and talking. At other times we remained silent, stretched out, under the trees. "I can't find work," he would say to me, pensively, worriedly. And I, the egotist, did not understand his words: "No one wants to give me work. They tell me: 'Go back to the monks.' But I can't leave my mother and younger brother and sister alone."

He had more free time than during the summer, but he was serious, preoccupied. Seated on the stairs, he would play distractedly with a blue stone, which he always carried in his pocket. Antonia said: "Malene's boy, the big one, could do worse than return to the convent. As it is, he's eating himself alive . . . They'll make a vagabond of him. He'll end up badly."

One day my cousin told me:

"You're no longer in our gang."

I shrugged my shoulders. He added:

"You have your friends still, don't you?"

"Yes."

"And Jorge, he's a friend of yours?"

"A great friend," I answered. "The friendliest of all my friends."

He pulled my ribbon off, and stood, twirling it on his index finger, looking at me with his pale green eyes.

It was time for mathematics. The Chink said:

"Leave these matters for later. Now study."

But I was lying. Jorge still seemed far off, fearful to me, and even if he attracted me, I felt ashamed of the idea of returning to Son Major.

One market day I met Sanamo, a basket over his arm. From the corner of Santa María the hubbub of the vendors could be heard. Sanamo had bought a round mirror, which he smilingly showed me, making its reflection run along the church wall and flinging it at me, against my eyes.

"Won't you all come back up there, my pigeons? Don't you want to have a snack again with the master?"

"Maybe." I raised my head, so that he might not notice my confusion.

"Maybe, any day," he echoed.

He went off laughing, and I, my pride injured, ran to fetch Manuel. I took a long time in finding him. I waited for him more than an hour at the door of his orchard.

"Manuel, why don't we go back to Son Major?"

He looked at the ground. His humble attitude touched and irritated me at the same time:

"Don't look at the ground, hypocrite! The monks taught you that, didn't they? . . . We're going to Son Major again! The old man is tempting us!"

"I can't go, you know it. Don't ask me to go."

I fell silent, because I was really afraid. We sat down very close to one another on the steps of his porch. We were in the habit of holding hands, and we remained that way a long time, without talking. He put his little blue stone, burnished with so much caressing, between our two hands, and the two of us held it, squeezed between our palms. It was like sharing a secret. No one could have understood this more than he. We scarcely moved, our hands stuck together, feeling the slight pain of the little stone. He was looking straight out in front of him, over the tops of the trees. With his free hand, he picked up a twig and traced lines on the ground. We could spend a long time this way, and we created so much heat in our hands that it was as if we had brought them close to a fire. Sometimes we carried the blue stone to one of our cheeks, and it seemed to burn.

We were like this, speechless, our hands intertwined, when a grey stone came over the wall and fell at our side. We heard stifled laughs, and then Guiem and the cripple crossed in front of the door. We watched them run toward the rocks. Sebastián, limping, carried a whip raised over his head as if it were a flag.

The following day, after five o'clock class, my cousin said to me, while he was pulling his sweater down over his head:

"You're not coming with me."

"No?" I laughed.

"No, I already told you that you weren't part of our gang. No need to get mad, you know . . . there can be days of truce from time to time."

"Ah, very well. So I have to be in Guiem's gang now?"

"Well no . . . It seems to me Guiem is coming over to our gang. And the cripple too . . . The things that happen!"

"Do what you want. I didn't want to be in your gang anyway! You're all too dull."

"I already figured as much. A girl like you gets bored with our doings . . . You have other ways of amusing yourself!"

He screwed up his mouth in order to say it, and smoothed down the hair mussed when he put on his sweater.

I did not understand what he meant, but I felt a certain worry.

"Son Major is very pretty," I said, hoping to awake his jealousy.

He turned red, and went away, shrugging his shoulders. But I guessed that with the last phrase I had cut him to the quick. I felt strangely cheated: I did not know by what or by whom. I could not imagine where Manuel was, nor did I want to see him. I followed Borja at a distance, dallying along the road, so as to stay hidden. He went down the Descent by leaps and bounds, until he was lost from sight in the direction of the dock. "No, not that," I told myself. I could not bear his taking Guiem's gang to the *Young Simón:* with our secrets, with the Andersen book of tales hidden there, with grandfather's Cuban cigars in their cedar boxes, with our carbine, with everything of Borja's and mine alone, treasures not even permitted to Juan Antonio. He couldn't do that. Juan Antonio and the administrator's children had returned to their schools in the city. And I was alone, completely alone. And Manuel . . . "Ah, but Manuel," I told myself, as if awaking from a dream that up until then had lulled me, "he isn't like us. He doesn't count in these things!" Perhaps he was too good. (His timid smile and

those words in the cold of the morning: "Caucasus,"
"Ukraine," "Ionian Sea" . . . And when I would say to
him: "Why does the Little Mermaid want an immortal
soul so much?" he would not answer, or perhaps he
would graze my hair gently.) He was not like us, not like
the men. He was something apart. It could not be. And
Jorge . . . It hurt me so much to think about him! I
squeezed my chest with my hand when I pronounced
his name. Under my sweater was the gold medal. "I'll
put it around his neck and I'll say: take this, it's something of mine." (But I did not know if it would be for
Jorge, Manuel, or perhaps even Borja.) "And those louts
will poke around and manhandle our treasures. *The
Traveling Companion,* read by Guiem? It's not possible!
He'd ask: 'What's this good for?' Or maybe: 'And this,
what does it mean?'" And Borja would shrug his shoulders. Probably they will try the carbine, and . . . Was it
jealousy, selfishness? A very sharp pain made my heart
beat faster. "No, not that bunch. Not them."

I sat down next to the well. Then I saw Malene, wearing a pink and grey handkerchief around her head, come
into view. Her long white neck emerged resplendent,
and her blue eyes had a green brilliance, like the sea. From
down below a light haze spread slowly up the Descent.

Malene was carrying a basket made of palm and she
seemed to be coming from the village. I turned my eyes
away from her, and felt a strange shame. "Underneath the
handkerchief her hair is scarcely grown back . . . all
soft and tawny." It made Guiem and the villagers laugh;
they also whistled at her from a distance, and even in-

sulted her. Malene went into the orchard, and did something she had never done before: she closed the door, and it squeaked on its hinges. I stood on tiptoe and leaned half my body over the wall. Malene went up the stairs and into the house. I think that until that minute I had never seen a woman more beautiful or proud.

Two days later—and I remember it distinctly—I again saw Manuel, who was coming from the forge. As a final gesture, he went to ask Guiem's father for work. (He had already been to the wagoner, the shoemaker, and the baker.) He was walking toward me, through the artisans' street, and the sun—a pale, glowing sun—haloed his head in gold. His left hand was stuck in his pocket, and with his right hand, he was pushing his lapels up around his throat. I said to him:

"Come with me."

"Don't make me go there, again . . . !"

"No, not there. To the *Young Simón.*"

Sometimes I had talked very vaguely about the old boat, and as he never asked any questions, I confided in him.

"Now? . . ."

His time was not like mine, and perhaps he could not follow me just then. But I was selfish and did not reflect on anything. And I knew that in the end he would go wherever I might ask. Even to Son Major.

He probably had other tasks, or, at least, something on his mind which tormented him and held him aloof. Perhaps he was waiting for his mother, or his brother and sister . . . Then, how I wanted to tear out all his affection for everyone else, to set him apart from the whole world! A gloomy sadness, perhaps evil, overcame me when I discovered him so attached to his family. I would have wanted him estranged from the whole world—even from me—before knowing him to be tied to someone who was not I. But he followed me without saying anything. I do not believe I have known anyone less talkative than that poor boy. It is possible that the greater part of our meetings were reduced almost always to a monologue on my part, or to a long, warm and inexplicable silence, which brought us closer together than any words could.

We rowed to Santa Catalina in a cold wind. When we landed, the gold shells crunched under our feet. It was December already, and the sky was pale.

I remember that I told him, rubbing my knees the while:

"I would like it to snow. Have you ever seen snow?"

"No, I've never seen it."

The water was beating against the rocks, and the *Young Simón* seemed blackish, almost sinister. Our faces were red and our eyes tearing. The wind whipped my hair, like a black flag. I jumped over the *Young Simón,* banging against the deck with my feet. He began to laugh, and I thought I had never heard a laugh like that. I opened the hatchway and rummaged around the belly of the boat. There were our treasures. All wrapped up, still, in Borja's old raincoat.

But Manuel did not show any interest in all that. When I spoke to him or showed him something, he would say only:

"Yes, yes," absent-mindedly.

We sat for a while on the gunwale of the *Young Simón,* our legs hanging over. It was cold, and we rubbed our hands together to warm up. I asked him:

"Do you like the things I showed you?" And he said only:

"Yes."

"But say it in another way!"

He sat looking at me, serious and silent. I thought: "He never talks about himself, he never tells me things about himself." But I did not want to ask him anything. Perhaps because he might say something that would tear off, even if only a corner, a part of the curtain that separated us from the world. My cowardliness was only comparable to my selfishness.

Then we heard Borja's voice calling us; he had made a horn with his hands. How tall he seemed to me, suddenly, on the rock, in long pants.

"Borja!"

I think I went pale. I had just betrayed our secret, and I was not sure—far from it—that he had betrayed it earlier to Guiem. I jumped from the boat. Manuel did not move.

Borja began to climb down the rocks. He always said it was very dangerous to climb around through that place, the place from which José Taronjí had thrown himself in his desire to escape. And at that moment,

I realized: "How thick and unfeeling of me. Here's where José Taronjí died, and I made Manuel . . ." The holes from the bullets could still be seen. And I had insisted he sit down on top of them. But Manuel remained as always, serene and silent. "Yes, he's too good, he's irritatingly good," I thought uneasily.

Borja came up to us. I expected to see him furious, but he did not say anything. Just the opposite, he was smiling. (It was the same smile he bestowed on grandmother every morning.) I understood, by that smile, that he had definitely placed me on the other side of the barrier. Because of that, I felt a stinging melancholy. He said:

"You bring your friends here? . . . Seems all right to me."

Then he sat down and offered us cigarettes. Manuel did not smoke and I hypocritically refused. Borja began to talk of silly things. Then he fell silent. And then he said:

"It's cold."

He went to the edge of the sea and stood there looking at it for a moment. It really was a cold day. The water was a dark grey. There was something in the waves like a restrained threat. Borja crouched, filled his hands with golden shells and returned toward us, depositing them with care on the *Young Simón*. He amused himself for a few minutes by arranging them by size. We were watching him do this with the interest that slightly ridiculous and minor things awaken in one at times.

Unexpectedly, he lifted his head, and his eyes were so desolate, I was shocked.

"Manuel," he said. "Listen to me, Manuel, do you want to do me a favor?"

I opened my mouth and closed it again. I wanted to intervene between that request and my friend, but I did not know what to say. Manuel leaned against the boat, exactly where the bullet-holes were. Borja came closer to him and put his hand on his arm:

"Manuel," he insisted. "You know . . . All the awful things I might have said to you were only foolishness . . . Really, I'm your friend. Do you know something? You're better than Juan Antonio. I've always liked you better . . . But you don't seem to know it, and . . . well, probably I haven't shown it."

Manuel looked straight ahead of him, with an expression I did not recognize.

Borja went on, hurriedly and incoherent:

"I'm asking you a favor. It's very important for me and for Matia, too . . . If not, I wouldn't have looked for you. Matia, do you know? . . . grandmother has found out about the *Young Simón*. Someone gave away the secret. Maybe it was the Chink, since they're going to get rid of him! . . . Well, I don't know, but it's all the same. Whoever it is will pay for it, in any case. Now Matia, you know how important it is for us! Isn't it? It's only that grandmother shouldn't find out, she shouldn't find anything here . . . !"

It seemed to me that an almost furious sadness shone in Manuel's eyes again, a sadness I discovered by surprise one day, or perhaps a contempt for the fact that he was beyond us, that he was passing, even, beyond himself. At that moment he looked amazingly like Jorge of Son Major, and in his face, so young still, there was almost the same weariness, the same jaded quality. Standing so close to him, my cousin seemed insignificant, wispy. And once again I thought: "If he wanted, he could throw Borja on the ground with a single blow."

"What's the matter with you?" interrupted Manuel, brusquely. "What is it you want?"

Borja made a strange gesture with his hands which reminded me of grandmother.

"Very well . . . don't ask me to explain it to you in detail. Matia either . . . isn't that so, Matia . . . ? If grandmother finds out . . . and she'll find out, because she'll examine this . . . I'm asking you to take my boat, and row it to the Port; and to turn over what I'm going to give you to Mariné. You know him, don't you?"

"Yes," Manuel answered dryly.

"You give it to him and tell him: 'Keep this for me.' We'll go and pick it up when there's no danger. There, it will be safe, and you'll save Matia and me from grandmother's rage . . ."

I was surprised, I couldn't make it out. Borja jumped aboard the *Young Simón,* extracted the wrapped-up raincoat and took out a box of money he had stolen from grandmother and Aunt Emilia. He shined up the box, rubbed it with a pensive air and held it out to Manuel:

"Take it to Mariné . . . and don't talk to him about me, he's a bit of a blabberer. Tell him: 'Keep it for me, I'll come for it.'"

Manuel contemplated the box without a move.

"Don't tell me you don't want to now . . . I beg you, Manuel! It's so important for us! I could only trust you. I don't trust the other guys at all . . . Besides, perhaps you don't remember that once, right here . . . you asked me for the boat and I lent it to you?"

When he heard this, something seemed to shake Manuel. Borja backed away slightly. Manuel pulled the box from his hands, and without saying anything made his way to the *Leontina*. Borja followed him, shaking the sand from his pants. But he was very excited, as if he had run a great deal.

"He should keep it! Do you hear? He should just keep it . . ."

"Shut up," Manuel said sharply.

Borja obeyed him. We saw him disappear in silence, as on that other day. I, too, as on that other day, looked at my cousin out of the corner of my eye, and I saw that his lips were drained of color.

Just like that other time, we walked back home along the rocks of the cliff.

3

I did not see Manuel again. The days followed one another rapidly, and the Christmas holidays were suddenly upon us. We received more definitive news of Uncle Álvaro and the war. Grandmother made up packages for the village poor. It was the first wartime Christmas, and grandmother said it should be marked by sobriety.

However, Lorenza and Antonia worked vigorously in the stifling kitchen. And I remember, as in a steamy lethargy, the endless meals grandmother ordered served during those days. We spent at least half of our time between the table and church. We went to church light-headed from the vapors of the kitchen, and there our heads were filled with canticles, shining lights and incense, so that we might again return to the obligations of the table. (It was odd, compared to the Christmases I had spent with Mauricia, in the country. We would pick holly branches and set up a crèche of clay figures, painted in garish colors, which she had bought for me in the market.)

Monsignor Mayol appeared in all his glory during those days. Grandmother was right, when she said that there was something of the prince about him. For the Christmas Eve dinner Monsignor Mayol, the vicar, the doctor—who was a widower—and Juan Antonio (who had just arrived from school to spend the vacation with his father) all gathered to eat at our house. The administrator and his wife, León, Carlos, and another priest (not a native of the island) who came to officiate at midnight Mass, were also present.

Santa María was resplendent. Monsignor Mayol, tall and exquisite, followed by his two acolytes, was dressed in the palest of pink, and in gold and pearls. The girls and boys of the confraternity sang in the choir. The brilliance of it all blinded one's eyes. Borja and I leaned our shoulders one against the other. It seemed to me he had drunk too much; his eyes kept closing. Monsignor Mayol raised his hands slowly, as solemn as an angel, and his head shone silvery.

Christmas Day was rather sad. Antonia asked me:

"Did you say a prayer for your mother yesterday?"

"That's my affair," I answered.

But the truth was that my conscience worried me, because I did not remember her at all. Only for a moment, during supper, did I think of my father. "How strange that I'm always so far from him, but I do remember things about him: the odor of his cigarettes, his hoarseness, something he said." Where could he be? What could he be doing?

On Christmas afternoon the old maids from Son Lluch, wearing their awful hats, came to the house along with Monsignor Mayol, the vicar and the other priest. The inevitable doctor, Juan Antonio, and the administrator's children were also there. "Always the same, always the same people." Borja and Juan Antonio talked about school, the same one Borja would go to after the holidays. They were together, at least, while . . .

"What's the name of my school?" I asked grandmother spiritlessly.

"It's a good boarding school," she responded laconically, so as to annoy me.

On Saint Stephen's Day I went down the Descent for a while to see if Manuel might be there. I did not see him and I sat down next to the wall of his orchard, playing with pebbles, until Antonia called me.

Grandmother was asking for Borja and me, to tell us:

"Lauro is going to the front, the same day you both go off to school."

"But didn't you say he wasn't fit for service?" my cousin asked, surprised. "He has bad eyes . . . that's why they threw him out of the Seminary . . ."

"Now it doesn't matter," grandmother said.

And she added:

"I want you to go and congratulate him."

We obeyed bad-humoredly. Lauro was with his mother, in the sewing room. Embarrassed, we hovered at the door. Seated on a low chair, Antonia was marking heaps of Borja's clothes and mine with red thread. From behind his green glasses, the Chink watched her. Gondoliero was flying from one side to another, mumbling: "Lauro, Lauro, Lauro . . . Pretty parakeet." The bird was bustling nervously on her head, on her shoulder. Neither the mother nor son said anything at all. Lauro was seated, his arms around his knees. No one seemed less heroic than he. My cousin spoke first:

"Lauro, grandmother says you're going to the front."

The Chink got up slowly. With his index finger he pushed up the frame of his glasses. Antonia remained motionless, her head bent down. Between her hands, she held one of the hideous nightgowns I used in Our Lady of the Angels. With the point of her scissors she was pulling out the numbers and letters embroidered on the shoulder, in order to replace them with others.

"Perhaps you'll see my father . . ." my cousin said.

The Chink remained silent. I did not look at him. I

could only see the point of Antonia's scissors, which glittered cruelly over the white clothes.

"Well, Lauro, grandmother says we must congratulate you."

From above the scissors, upon my vanished numbers, something wet and shining fell, like a drop. I turned and ran toward my room. As if I wanted to hide something, and without knowing the reason why, I looked for my almost forgotten Gorogó. I did not find him.

On the morning of the Feast of the Three Kings, grandmother gave us our gifts: books, a couple of fountain pens, sweaters, and things like that. The happiness of toys was finished forever, and gifts began to be a problem, according to grandmother and Aunt Emilia. (Mauricia would put my shoe in the hollow of the fireplace. As it was not enough for me, she wove an enormous stocking with loose wool, which turned out to be a "Joseph's cloak of many colors." And there, all the gifts which my father sent would be converted into the gift from the Three Wise Men of the East. Days before, if I would see elongated clouds, I would ask: "Mauri, tell me, is that the road from the East?" One year they brought me a clown as big as myself, and I hugged it. But why remember that?)

We took grandmother's gifts, and kissed her. Aunt Emilia gave me a bottle of French perfume, one she had kept unopened. "Now you're a woman," she said. And she also kissed me. (Everybody kissed one another a great deal during those days.)

No one in the house went without a gift. Monsignor Mayol, the vicar, Juan Antonio . . . Carlos and León received a bicycle for both of them. (And everybody shared it.)

Loaded down with our books, Borja and I went to the study room. We settled into the facing armchairs, next to the balcony. The sun felt warm through the glass. An unseasonable fly buzzed awkwardly from one side to the other.

Borja was collapsed in his chair. It was very roomy and upholstered in leather, with scratches, and dark stains in many places. He threw a leg over one of the arms of the chair, and swung it.

My books were not worth much. Aunt Emilia had picked them out.

Since the meeting in Santa Catalina, Borja treated me almost as he did grandmother. We did not fight again.

I noticed that he would look at me over his open book. His pale green pupils looked like hollow glass. ("The look reserved for grandmother.") I made a face at him. He laughed behind the book and said:

"Do you know something?"

"What do I have to know?"

He threw his book on the floor and stretched his arms, yawning falsely:

"That I have you in the palm of my hand."

I managed to screw up my lips scornfully, but my heart began to beat hard.

"Don't make idiotic faces; I've got you in my hands,

just like Lauro and Juan Antonio. And everyone else, in the end! You know me by now, I know everything. Everything that should be known!"

I feigned indifference and picked up my books again. He added:

"Very well, you've got nothing to be afraid of if you're a good girl."

"I'll be what I want to be, you idiotic monkey."

"No; you won't be what you want to be. Because . . ."

He shut up, acting mysterious, and looking at me with all the malice that could possibly fit in his eyes.

"If I were to tell . . . do you know what would happen to you?"

"And what do you have to tell, stupid? I know more things about you!"

"Bah, boyish pranks! Yours is worse! They'd put you in a reform school for being a pervert. 'The rotten apple might ruin the sound ones,' and all that. Go on, if you think we don't know everything! Juan Antonio and even Guiem . . . We've seen you."

"Who?"

"You and your friends. It was very amusing spying on you. Guiem and Ramón . . . and Juan Antonio and I . . . Well, why should I tell you? You know it yourself. A fourteen-year-old with two lovers! They'd put you in a reform school . . ."

"Me, no . . ."

Carefully, Borja unscrewed the cap of his fountain pen and examined the point as if it were something precious.

I was surprised. More surprised, perhaps, than scared.

"Don't act as if you're innocent now! You, yourself, said many times that I was just a boy next to you, that you knew much more than I . . . And damned if it didn't turn out to be true! You dirty . . . !"

Again he laughed wickedly.

"Yes, yes; the two of you together, there, in the orchard, and on the Descent . . . And then, at Son Major! With the old fellow, too, isn't that so?"

"We never went back to Son Major! That's a lie!"

"No, eh? . . . You said it yourself! And Sanamo too . . ."

"Sanamo is an old liar . . ."

"Very well, we won't discuss it. I have as many witnesses as I want. Do you know what a reform school is? I'm going to tell you. You always go around saying you like trees, flowers, and all that . . . well, then never, never again will you see trees, flowers, and you'll almost never see the sun . . . Because, on top of everything else, you've a bad past: your father . . ."

I got up and grabbed his arm. I would have slapped him, hit him, kicked him—if I had not been so scared. In one fell swoop the subtle haze, the curtain, which separated me from the world, was torn away. In one brutal stroke, everything I struggled not to know was upon me.

"Dirty liar . . . Don't talk to me about my father!"

He pushed me away blandly.

"Don't get excited. It's not good for you. Your father's

a filthy red, who, perhaps at this very moment, is shooting at my father. Do you remember what happened to José Taronjí?"

I sat down. I was very cold and my knees trembled. (Oh, how cruel, how pitiless, how gullible a fourteen-year-old can be.)

"You're in my power. I've read up on reform schools. There are punishment cells. And it seems to me that you . . ."

He continued talking, and I closed my eyes. The buzz of the fly went on. A winter fly that probably had lost his comrades. Through my eyelids I could see the sun turn red. I felt the rough leather of the armchair on the palms of my hand. How much Borja knew about reform schools; I never would have imagined it!

I babbled:

"It isn't true! We were there, yes, on the ground . . . but we only held hands, and never . . ."

How could I talk to him about the little blue stone, how could I tell him that everything he accused me of was beyond his understanding?

"Of course, if you're a good girl nothing will happen to you. Look at the Chink: he never turned on me, he did what I wanted . . . and grandmother didn't find out about the Naranjal."

"You don't tell the truth, Borja . . ."

"I have witnesses."

I vaguely remembered Guiem and the cripple, throwing a stone at us from across the wall, and running down the Descent with a whip held high.

"You won't do that . . ."

Borja had won and I had lost. I, a stupid braggart, an ignorant creature, had lost.

Aunt Emilia came in.

"What are you doing here so quiet? Why don't you go out in the garden for a while? The sun is shining as if it were spring. Take advantage of it! Nobody understands you: you go out when the wind is howling, and now you stay indoors, locked up. Go on, take advantage of it, it's the last day of vacation!"

The last day, that was true.

After lunch, Borja called me with a gesture. I followed him, bursting with cowardliness, hating myself.

"Matia, I'm going to confess. Come on with me to Santa María."

"I don't have to confess."

"Are you sure? Very well, it's your conscience. But come with me."

I followed him. I would follow him in everything, from that moment on. I began to understand the Chink, and I was filled with something like remorse. "If the Chink was terrorized by this slippery fellow, how did I expect not to be, stupid chatterbox and fool that I am?"

We bundled up and went out of the house. He took me by the hand, as in our better days. We crossed the garden. The fig tree was bare, with its silvery branches reaching toward the sky. There was something in that wintry sun which was repeating: "the last day," or "the last time." At the end of the street, like an engraving in my book of Andersen's tales, shone the green-gold cupola of Santa María.

We went to church. Borja wet his fingers in the holy water, and, extending his hand toward me, dampened mine. Saint George stood out in the darkness, his lance nailed in the dragon. A gold circle glistened around his helmet. Tiny, ruby-colored rhomboids bordering the stained-glass window were like the wine in wine glasses. The lamp seemed to rock gently. Something settled on my heart, striking into me with its small claws like a black Gondoliero. A man was kneeling next to the altar, his face between his hands. It was the Chink.

"Is he crying?" I asked Borja.

My cousin kneeled next to me, his arms crossed over his chest. He whispered:

"He doesn't believe in anything!"

But there was the Chink, afflicted, under the stained-glass windows he loved so much. I contemplated his narrow shoulders stuffed into his black jacket. I said to myself: "They'll probably kill him at the front, probably put a bullet through him in that posture, through his back."

(And that is what happened. A month later, he was killed. And his mother, who did not know it, got up earlier than usual that day, and when she went to give Gondoliero his food she saw that the bird would not eat. When she served grandmother breakfast, she said: "Señora, Lauro is going to come, I am sure of it. My heart tells me he is going to come." But he was killed at that very hour, and Antonia went on serving breakfast,

feeding the blue and brilliant Gondoliero, who was repeating: "Pretty parakeet, pretty parakeet." Lorenza told
me all this years later, when things were very different.)

Borja crossed himself and lowered his head. I looked
around me on all sides, half-closing my eyes. Through
my eyelashes the stained-glass windows were winking,
casting lights.

Borja entered the sacristy, and in a little while came
out again. He held his hands together, his head lowered.
He seemed mysterious to me, and my nervousness in-
creased as I watched him. A little later, Monsignor Mayol
himself came out, wrapping his stole around his neck.
He entered the confessional, and Borja went toward
him. He stuck his head between the purple curtains,
and Monsignor Mayol's arm encircled his shoulders
lovingly. They were like that a long time. The hard
board of the bench pressed into my knees. The Child
Christ wore a green velvet tunic, with embroidery and
gold lace. One of the wooden fingers on his right hand
was split open, and his big enamel eyes stared fixedly.
The little saint in the stained-glass window, with his
chestnut-colored skirt and his long gilded feet, monopo-
lized all the sunlight. Saint George, on the other hand,
had paled. Outside, the wind began to blow, and, suddenly, a cloud blinded everything. Something crossed
the nave, flying clumsily. "It's a bat," I told myself. It
bounced against the walls, and fell in a corner, limp,
like a black rag. It smelled moldy in there. The big
ribs of the nave, like a boat submerged in the sea, covered
with moss, gold and shadows, exuded something fas-

cinating and oppressive. I felt tired: "Oh, if only I'd never have to leave here," I thought. I did not have any desire to live. Life seemed long and useless to me. I felt such hatred, such indifference to everything, that even the air, the light of the sun, and the flowers seemed foreign to me.

Borja returned:

"Aren't you going to make confession?" he asked.

"I don't have any sins to confess."

He looked at me in an odd way.

"Come on."

I got up. Borja bent a knee before the Host, and Monsignor Mayol signaled us to wait. We went out and sat down on the stone stairway to wait for him.

"Why is Monsignor Mayol coming with us?"

"I've asked him to."

The wind grew more violent and the clouds were covering over the sun which had looked so beautiful in the morning. At last Monsignor Mayol came out and we went back home.

"Grandmother, may we speak with you?"

Grandmother, pale and spongy, was in her boudoir rocking chair. She looked stupefied at Borja and Monsignor Mayol. Then, with a weary gesture she indicated the armchair in front of her.

I wanted to set off at a run, to escape to some place where fear would not imprison me. But Borja took me by the hand:

"Stay here, Matia."

His lips trembled.

"No . . ." I protested weakly.

"Stay, if Borja wants you to!" decided the icy voice of the parish priest.

I stood up, behind Monsignor Mayol's armchair. Borja advanced as far as grandmother and kneeled. I could only see grandmother's face, her round owl's eyes rimmed with dark circles, and her mouth busy chewing something. The ring glittered on her hand like an evil eye which would outlive our corruption. Monsignor Mayol said:

"Doña Práxedes, Borja wants to make a confession to you."

Grandmother remained silent for a moment. Then the pill crumbling between her teeth could be heard. And she said coldly:

"Get up, boy."

But Borja did not get up. His head was lowered, and over his shiny hair emerged the top half of grandmother's body: on her right were the dethroned opera glasses, surely accustomed already to many farces.

The boy said:

"Grandmother, I come to ask your forgiveness. I've already confessed, but I want you to forgive me too. I couldn't live without confessing to you . . . Grandmother, I . . ."

And he began to cry. His weeping was strange. With his face between his hands, he was crying silently, as on that afternoon in the Son Major garden, when we did not know if it were sorrow or a simple headache which overcame him.

"Well," said grandmother, as she stopped chewing. "Go on."

Borja uncovered his face. A face I did not see, but which I knew was without tears. And he said, in a rush:

"I've taken advantage of you, I've cheated you . . . I've been stealing from you. I've stolen money, a lot of money, and . . ."

Grandmother raised her eyebrows. It seemed to me that her chest swelled like a wave.

"Ah," she said serenely. "So it was you, eh?"

I could have sworn she was not aware of it, but apparently she knew.

"Yes, I did it . . . And I wanted to get it back and return it to you. But I can't, I don't have it any longer!"

"To whom did you give it?" said grandmother, cleaning the binoculars with a handkerchief.

Borja lowered his head.

At that moment it hurt me to know everything. (The knowledge of the dark life of grownups, to whom, without any doubt, I now belonged. It hurt me and I felt a physical pain.)

"I couldn't help it, grandmother . . . forgive me. The first time I was to blame: I bet with him . . . But the other times . . . Forgive me, grandmother, I've suffered so much! Good God, I've paid for it dearly! He had me in his power; he was threatening me, he said he'd come

and tell you if I didn't give him more and more . . . I
didn't want to, but he said that if we didn't go on he'd
tell on me . . . It was horrible. I couldn't live. And it's
because he had to get money together, he said, in order
to buy himself a boat to sail to the Greek islands. He's
crazy, yes, crazy! 'You'll never be able to make it,' I
told him. 'They're so far away.' But he'd answer that
what I told him were only pretexts so as not to give him
more money . . . He's a devil, like a devil . . . He'd
hit me if I didn't obey . . . He's much stronger than I!"

He rolled up his sweater sleeve, sobbing like a wretched
little slut, and displayed the wound from the butcher
hook. Coldly, grandmother raised her hand and cut him
off:

"Who?"

I could not bear any more. I turned and fled. I opened
the door and ran down the staircase. At the end of the
corridor stood the clock with its tic-toc. "They mustn't
find him," I said to myself. "They musn't find him. He
must escape, get away . . ."

I went out to the Descent. The wind went on groaning
and I leaned up against the wall. Among the almond
trees rose the white and greenish mist. There below, the
pitas stood straight up like shrieks.

Manuel's orchard was a few yards further on, but I
did not dare get closer. Something was hurting me so
much that I could not stir. The wind mixed cruelly with
the earth, with the grass, still green and alive. Two
papers whirled along, pursuing one another. From where

I was standing the olive trees in Manuel's orchard looked like livid green stains. A pearl-white brilliance, like clean smoke, ascended from the sea.

An enormous cowardice held me fast to the ground. "You know, you won't see the sun and the flowers, and all the other things you like so much . . . And your father" . . . (Oh, the crystal ball which snowed inside. Did I really like the flowers, and sun, and trees so much? And the Chink, crying in church . . .) The outside of my body shivered, but the cold inside me was even greater.

Ton came out. They had sent word to look for the boy. I knew they had ordered Ton to look for him. And I did not even have the strength to tell him: "Don't go, Ton, say that you can't find him, tell him to get away." (Because there was only one voice shaking me: "Coward, traitor, coward.")

He pulled him out from among the olive trees, it seemed. From among the silver-green olive trees, he brought him: as from the haze, among the tree trunks, toward me. Yes, he came toward me. The poor boy was going toward no one else. Ton was dragging him along, grasping him by the arm.

As he passed, he looked at me. I could do nothing else but follow him, like a dog, breathing my betrayal, without daring even to flee. I followed his steps to grand-mother's boudoir. (The creaking of the staircase, the tic-toc of the clock, there in the corner, as at the siesta hour, when I said to him: "It seems awful what they're doing to all of you." And what we were throwing in his well

was a thousand times worse than a dead dog, I thought.)
I stopped behind the half-closed door of the boudoir,
and Ton and Antonia—who had followed us, fascinated
—stood by my side, behind the curtain, listening. Hearing
him say, say only:

"No . . . no . . ."

The worst of it all was his silence.

Borja, on the other hand, was crying and moaning:
"To sail to the Greek islands, like his . . . !"

Monsignor Mayol's voice interrupted him, forcing him
to be silent.

They sent Ton to the Port with the boat. He returned
with the box of money. His clouded white eye shone
like a phosphorescent snail.

I do not know how I reached the pier. My clothes were
soaked in the spume of the sea. Ton looked at me, as he
jumped from the boat.

"You've done very well by him, very well. They'll
send him off to a reformatory! What good intentions!"

(Neither the light, nor the sun, nor the trees mattered
to me. How, then, could I leave him without light, trees,
and sun?)

They took him away from there, between Monsignor
Mayol and the younger Taronjí, cousin of his father,
José. "He's too young," said Lorenza, "to be put in
prison." They knew already, then, where they were
taking him. "Where?" I asked. And nothing ever gave
me so much fear as their silence and their ignorance.
(The word *reformatory,* how unusually well Ton knew
how to pronounce it!)

I do not know how the day ended. I do not remember how supper was gotten through, nor what Borja talked of, nor I. I do not remember, even, how or when we said goodbye to the Chink.

I only know that at dawn, I was awakened. That, as on the first day of my arrival on the island, the pearled grey light of dawn slashed across the green shutters of my window. My eyes were open. For the first time, I had not dreamed of anything. There was something in the room like a beating of pigeon wings in flight. Then I realized that at one point in the afternoon—as the light was dying—I had returned there, that I had remained a prisoner of the wind, next to the green, locked iron gate of Son Major. I called Jorge, desperately, but only Sanamo appeared, his keys jingling, saying, "Come in, come in, little pigeon." His grey hair rose in the wind, he was indicating the closed balcony. And he said: "He's up there." I screamed to him: "They're going to punish Manuel, and he's innocent." But the balcony remained closed, and no one answered, nor spoke, nor was any voice heard at all. And Sanamo was laughing. It was as if no one had been in that house, as if it had never even existed, as if we had invented all of it. Out of breath, I returned home and looked for Aunt Emilia, and I told her: "What Borja said isn't true . . . Manuel's innocent." But Aunt Emilia looked through the window, as always. She turned, with her spongy smile, with her big jaws like white velvet, and said: "Very well, very well, don't torment yourself. Thank God you're going to school, and all will go back to normal." "But we have been bad, awful, with Manuel . . ." And she answered: "Don't take it like that, you'll realize some day that these are childish things . . ." And, suddenly, there was the dawn, like a despicable, terrible reality. And I, with my eyes opened, as punishment. (The Island of Never-Never did not exist and the Little Mermaid did not achieve an immortal soul because men and women do not love each other, and she was left with a couple of useless legs, and transformed into sea spray.) Stories were horrible. Moreover, I had lost Gorogó—I do not know where, under what heap of handkerchiefs and socks. The suitcase was already closed, its straps fastened, without Gorogó. And the Chink must have already gotten up. And probably the imbecilic Gondoliero would be pecking at his ear, and would there be flowers, irritated, flaming red flowers, in the little room up there? And that photograph of a boy in friar's habit and sagging stockings, where would it be? The red lampshades, like dead eyes, would glow in the house, the house with its fleeing rats and hidden brown spiders poking around in the cracks. Grandmother, her gold table service, her pills . . . Maybe she'd never be able to close her eyes. "These things, they say, are the conscience."

As on that other day, I jumped out of bed. And in that raw wakefulness, so real, so grey, I went barefoot, opened the balcony and jumped to the loggia. There was Borja, wrapped in his coat, pale, looking at me. He was smoking the last *Muratti*.

The arches of the loggia outlined the haze of a sky scarcely illumined by a light born behind the mountains, where the charcoal burners would still be sleeping. Borja threw the cigarette on the floor and we went toward one another, as if pushed, and embraced. He began to cry, and cry—how could anyone cry that way? But I could not (it was a punishment, because he always despised Manuel, while I, didn't I probably love him?). I was stiff, frozen, squeezing him against me. I felt his tears rolling down my neck, under my pajamas. I looked into the garden, and behind the cherry trees I made out the fig tree, which, in that light, seemed white. There stood the cock of Son Major, with his angry eyes, like two buttons of fire. Straight and luminous, like a handful of lime, he shrieked—dawn was breaking—his horrible, strident song, which proclaimed, perhaps—how do I know?—some mysterious lost cause.